SHADOW RETREATS

Jennifer J. Morgan

Books by Jennifer J. Morgan

Libby Madsen Cozy Mysteries

Shadows in the Forest
Spa Shadows
Shadowed Treasures
Shadow Retreats
The Christmas Fairy - a holiday novella

SHADOW RETREATS

Libby Madsen Cozy Mysteries, Book 4

Jennifer J. Morgan

Secret Staircase Books

Shadow Retreats
Published by Secret Staircase Books, an imprint of
Columbine Publishing Group, LLC
PO Box 416, Angel Fire, NM 87710

Book layout and design by Secret Staircase Books
First trade paperback edition: December, 2022
First e-book edition: December, 2022

Publisher's Cataloging-in-Publication Data

Morgan, Jennifer J.
Shadow Retreats/ by Jennifer J. Morgan.
p. cm.
ISBN 978-1649141224 (paperback)
ISBN 978-1649141231 (e-book)

1. Libby Madsen (Fictitious character). 2. Arizona—Fiction.
3. Amateur sleuths—Fiction. 4. Women sleuths—Fiction. I. Title

Libby Madsen Cozy Mystery Series : Book 4.
Morgan, Jennifer J., Libby Madsen cozy mysteries.

BISAC : FICTION / Mystery & Detective.

813/.54

To my husband—

You are the most supportive man on this planet. No matter what is going on, you stop what you're doing and are fully there to support family. You've been my backbone this year while it felt as though parts of me were unraveling. You help me stay grounded and focused. You constantly remind me of what is actually important in life. You've consistently shown me what love and kindness looks like—you are the embodiment of it. Your encouragement means everything to me. Thank you for being you!

Acknowledgements

Thank you to everyone who encouraged me to start writing. My mom, my husband, my daughter, and several friends who have encouraged me along the way—Thank You! I am LOVING it! And, I feel the same as when I first began this process last year and five manuscripts ago—even if no one ever purchased one of my stories, I would still feel gratified writing them. Writing is therapeutic, creative, and definitely helps me to focus. Of course, I couldn't do it without my editors and also the beta readers who catch every missed word and punctuation mistake I've made. With so much gratitude to Susan, Sandra, Paula, Marcia, and Isobel. You are fantastic!

Now, Libby and Shadow, Greg, Alexis, and JJ are all dear friends of mine and I fully enjoy hanging out with them every day. Life doesn't get any better than that!

CHAPTER ONE

Early October and the searing heat of summer was behind us. At least the mornings and evenings had cooled, which had Shadow and me ramping up our jogging schedule again. My energetic pup adored our routine—every morning at six she was standing right next to my bed, staring at me and gently panting. The second my eyes opened, she would start that cute little hop-around she does when excited. She used to sleep in her crate with the door closed, but ever since our Utah vacation several weeks back, she convinced me to leave the door removed so she could come and go. I may rethink that the earlier she wakes me up; I may need to attach that door again.

I waved her off and rolled over; I wasn't ready quite yet.

Closing my eyes, I ventured back into my thoughts. It had been a busy September—my friends and I traveled through Utah in our RVs and accomplished several amazing hikes, mountain biking, and kayaking. We met the coolest elderly couple and that in itself was the largest adventure we've done. My heart still warmed thinking of our new friends, Eugene and Agatha Walker. Even though we had only known them a short time, they sure wormed their way into all of our hearts. Then I remembered, we needed to plan another Lake Powell trip soon. We had business to take care of. *Maybe we could get that done sometime later this month?*

My thoughts drifted further … our day spa business had taken off ever since the physical therapy unit started up. We received many massage referrals now from the onsite therapists who worked with rehabilitation patients. My days were full. I love my work so I was energized by the full schedule and helping rehab patients with their healing, too. However, I hadn't seen my boyfriend, Greg Lawson, since we'd returned from Utah. I've learned—long distance relationships are not easy. Even being only two hours away, we have found it difficult to break away from our respective careers to make time for each other. We talk frequently on the phone—but that only goes so far.

Then, there was Bella, my roommate whom I'd invited to stay with me last spring. She's the daughter of a former client of mine; she had gone missing and Shadow and I untangled the whole sordid mess. Poor girl, she'd been through a lot. Struggling in her early twenties—it was the least I could do to offer her a place to stay after living with her mother was no longer an option. She has been thriving ever since—studying for her Emergency Medical Technician certification, working full-time at the spa, and also finding solace exploring her spirituality. She and Alexis had joined up with a spiritual group called Love & Mercy. Their 'guru' holds meetings locally each week and occasionally they'll also join retreats in other locations too. I don't fully understand it; never really been my thing. Alexis is certified to teach meditation, and is always trying to convince me of its many benefits. Maybe. For now, though, I'm happy Bella seems to be enjoying herself and we couldn't be prouder of the progress she's made recovering from her serious childhood traumas.

Shadow's paws thumped the side of the bed, her tongue licked my hand that draped over the side. Then, there was the small whine and the sound of her tail swooshing fast. *It was time*.

"Okay girl … wanna go outside?" Oh boy, did she. Shadow ran circles combined with a bounce, and she didn't stop until we were outside in the backyard. There, she took off for the far end of the grass. Sniffing all over, she finally did her business and then we came back in to make coffee.

"Good morning!" Bella said, as we came in through the sliding glass door. She had beat us to the coffee machine; it was already brewing.

"Hey, that's smelling nice. Morning came too quick." I yawned and stretched, enjoying the aroma of fresh brewed coffee. "Better get my run in before I chicken out." I went to my room and rummaged through my exercise clothing. A lightweight t-shirt and my leggings would do this morning. Once I was changed, I grabbed Shadow's harness—we call it a bra, and she definitely knows it by that name. She'll even bring it to me if I ask her to go get 'her bra.' This morning she could hardly hold still for me to get it in place, but we managed and then set off for our run.

My neighborhood in northeast Mesa backs up to acres of state land with a myriad of desert trails to explore. We alternate between trail running in the wilderness and jogging through the neighborhood streets. Today was a trail run. The desert was full of wildlife running about. The cute little quail families were squawking that funny little chirping thing they do. I always imagine what they're saying to one another; it's clear that everyone in their little family knows what mom or dad is commanding because they hop right to it when told. The bunnies run from us when they see a huge black beast coming for them. Shadow wouldn't hurt a flea, but she does love a good bunny chase. We followed the trails for roughly two miles and then headed back, only slowing down when we were back in the neighborhood.

I unhooked Shadow's leash and she immediately ran toward her water dish in the kitchen. After setting the leash on the entryway table, I rounded the corner into the kitchen and heard Bella as she was saying goodbye to someone. She set her phone down angrily on the breakfast bar.

"What's wrong, sweetie?" I asked, pouring coffee into a mug.

"One of my friends from Mercy called, upset. She's considering leaving the organization; I'm worried."

"Why worried? You can still be friends, right?"

She nodded. "It's not only that. I'm concerned for *her*."

I looked at her quizzically. "As in, for her safety?"

She nodded again. Her eyes welled up.

"What's going on, Bella?"

"Uh. Well ..." She hesitated while pouring herself another mug. "You know ... never mind. I probably shouldn't say. She confided in me."

"Okay. But, know I'm here if you need to talk."

She gave me a small half-smile and turned toward her bedroom as I opened the fridge and pulled out some ingredients to fix breakfast. Eggs, spinach, garlic, and some sausage—I'd whip up an omelet before heading to work.

As I cooked the sausage, my thoughts went back to Bella. She had seemed upset; yes, I should respect her friend's privacy ... but now, of course, I was super curious what it was about. And, Bella doesn't need anyone else's drama in her life right now. Because of her difficult childhood, it wasn't a far stretch to think that she could easily be led into the wrong crowd. But, at the end of the day, she was in her twenties and I'm not her mother. *Stop being nosy.*

I heated the garlic in olive oil until fragrant, then added a huge handful of spinach watching it wilt down into a manageable portion. Pouring the beaten eggs on top of the spinach and garlic mixture, I realized that Shadow had left the room. She normally helps me cook—by laying on my feet and hoping I'll drop something.

After eating my omelet, I poured another cup of coffee and headed down the hallway to my room. Shadow was laying outside of Bella's door, giving me the most pitiful look before she got up and followed me to the bathroom. "I know, girl. I'm worried too. We'll check in with her later—gotta give her space."

CHAPTER TWO

As I pulled into my parking space at Dharma Inspired Day Spa, I saw that Brian had arrived too. Brian Gant was one of the physical therapists from Healing Solutions, the physical therapy (PT) business that now rents the other half of our building. Over the summer, the company had finished the full-size swimming pool, state-of-the-art gym, and therapy spas for their patients. The whole operation was spectacular—with a team of twelve therapists helping clients recover from their injuries—it was a great addition for us.

Brian, the curly ginger-headed man of average height, had become a good friend of mine. We have similar schedules so we often have lunch together in the business' shared kitchen space. He's slightly older than me, I suspected anyway—I've never asked specifically, but based on similar tastes in pop culture, I'd say somewhere in his mid-to-late thirties also. He was one of the therapists who had personally referred more of his patients to Dharma Inspired than any other. Of course, he knows what a great effect we have because he also regularly receives Ashiatsu.

"Good morning!" I said, as I stepped out of my car.

"Libby—Good morning! Aww, how's my favorite pup doing?" he asked, when he saw me opening the back door of my 4Runner to unload Shadow. She ran right over to him.

"Energetic as always!"

We walked up to the building and wished each other a great day before he turned to walk inside the Healing Solutions front door. I opened our spa door to find Bella at the front desk and Sage already waiting for me in the lobby.

"Good morning, ladies," I smiled to each. "See you in few minutes, Sage. Please, enjoy some relaxation time in the Serenity Room."

She nodded and headed into the locker rooms where she could get changed and leave her belongings in one of the bamboo lockers. Most of our clients arrive early to enjoy the calm in our relaxation room. With its soft lighting, relaxed music, and a remarkable assortment of herbal teas, it was nearly impossible to do anything but unwind.

I stepped into the office and found my business partner, Alexis Johnson, sitting at her desk already crunching numbers. She got up, walked around her desk, and enveloped me in a giant hug.

"How are you today, my friend?" she asked.

"Great run this morning. Shadow and I hit the trails and were able to get about four miles in. Felt great after such a long summer."

"Wow! That's fantastic. It's all I can do to get JJ, Joshua, and myself fed and out the door each morning. Now, with Joshua in kindergarten, it's quite the rush."

I don't have kids so I can't imagine what that's like, but hearing tales from my sister, Jordan, and from Lexi—well, it makes me wonder if I actually ever want kids. I don't know how these super moms do it.

"Hey, I was wondering if you had heard what was going on with Bella's friend from Mercy? I'm guessing it's Jill, but she wouldn't tell me much. Jill's the only one I've heard her talk about."

Alexis contemplated and then said, "I have no idea. That's strange, I saw Jill last night at a meditation session I led. She seemed fine to me."

"Hmm. Well, Bella started to tear up and cry earlier when I got back from my run. She'd hung up with someone on the phone, seemed upset. I asked her what it was about, but she didn't want to talk about it. Said she was concerned for one of her friends. I assume it was serious—enough to make her cry anyway."

"I'll try to learn more. Thanks for letting me know."

I set my laptop bag down on my desk and then took my lunch to the kitchen. There were several employees who had arrived for their shifts and everyone seemed backed up at the coffee station. I skirted around Kathleen to get to the refrigerator and put my lunch bag in.

Kathleen McConnell and Diane Frost were new massage therapists at our facility. We knew them from massage school years back and they graciously filled in for us during our recent trip to Utah. By the time we returned, they had become charmed by our clients and the business we had established. It was a no-brainer; we required full-time help—we had to hire them. They've been a great addition.

Kathleen specializes in relaxation therapies. She works with patients who suffer PTSD from their injuries. Many service men and women have found her techniques exactly what they need. Diane specializes in neuromuscular facilitation, which is an assisted stretching and massage technique. Then, of course, Alexis and I both specialize in Ashiatsu as well as Swedish forms of massage. Together the four of us have become a well-rounded team.

"I saw Sage come in when I got here," Kathleen started. "Ashiatsu for her today?"

"Yep, I think she's addicted now," I smiled. "But, don't worry, she'll schedule the relaxation massage soon … always does."

Then, Kathleen's eyes started teasing. "Saw *Brian* …"

Wondering about her emphasis on the tech's name, I said, "Yeah, I already said good morning to him walking in."

"I see you guys having lunch nearly every day. He's cute!" her flirting eyes blinked a couple times.

Ah, this is where she was going.

"Oh, no, Kathleen. Brian has become a good *friend*. But, nothing …"

She winked as she interrupted. "Ookay …" then she turned, "Hey, have a great day … I gotta get set up for my client." She left the room.

Is that what people are starting to talk about around here? My heart sunk. I have a boyfriend; I don't need the rumor mill starting over an innocent friendship. Just then, Brian walked into the kitchen.

"Hey, we meet again!" he laughed.

I said a few pleasantries and then rushed out—must get to my client, I explained.

* * *

After a morning full of appointments, I found Alexis back at her desk.

"How about we head to the park for some lunch? It's gorgeous outside." I tempted my friend to get away from the computer for a while. Her degree was in business management and, along with being a therapist, she was the brains behind our operation. Now that it'd grown so much this year, we both could work on work-life balance.

"You know, that sounds amazing. We haven't gone out for lunch in months!" She hopped up and grabbed her purse. "Plus, I had a little chat with Bella …" she teased.

Shadow agreed, too. She seemed to understand when the word 'park' was mentioned. We retrieved our lunch bags from the refrigerator before heading out to her Lexus parked right out front. I noticed on our way out of the kitchen the wounded look on Brian's face when he realized I wouldn't be joining him in the break room. I shrugged pointing ahead to Lexi as she led the way out.

We pulled up to Red Mountain Park and then walked the short distance to one of the ramadas where there were several picnic tables. The park was quiet on this Tuesday morning—I expected as much, with school in session again. Shadow wanted to go run, but I let her know we'd do that after lunch.

"So, what did Bella say…?" I prompted.

"Jill Walsh is the friend she's made at Mercy. This young girl—probably early twenties, similar to Bella—

started with the group as a quiet, shy, meek demeanor. I don't know what her trauma was, but she was definitely running from something—or someone. She's really taken to meditation and I thought she was becoming more self-confident and less shy." She stopped to take a sip of her water. "Bella shared that she's concerned because of several conversations where Jill seemed ... well, not herself. At least, out of character with the person Bella had come to know."

"How?"

"She mentioned she was thinking of getting a tattoo. I guess she's also been interested in one of the new guys there at the center—Joseph. He's quite a bit older."

"I don't know. Sounds like a twenty-something to me. What's odd about being interested in boys and tattoos?" Shrugging my shoulders, I popped a grape into my mouth.

"Yeah, that seems normal enough, but it is different for *her*."

"Bella mentioned something about her friend wanting to leave Mercy though, and she was afraid. Or, something along those lines…?"

"Hmmm. She didn't mention that to me, but I did get the distinct feeling that she was concerned about this older tech-mogul guy that Jill was fawning over. Maybe something happened there?"

"How much older is this dude? Tech-mogul…?" I inquired.

"Oh, Joseph ... he's probably early forties, if I had to guess. I'm not entirely sure what company he's with, but he's CEO of a successful tech-media firm. Apparently, he was sent to Mercy by the board of his company to get his, uh, *stuff* together."

My eyes lifted. "Oooh! Sounds like a scandal there…"

"Seems Type-A to me. Can't put his phone down. Guru Kali Patel always struggles to get him to concentrate on being present when we gather for meditation. He's definitely a distraction during most sessions."

"Guru…" I laughed. "Really?"

She laughed too. "I know, I know. You aren't into all this, and that's fine. But, I've got to tell you … Kali is the most peaceful, loving, spiritual person I've ever known. You've got to meet her. You'd love her presence, if nothing else … so peaceful. Looking at her, you *see* her aura. Strikingly lithe, stunning dark complexion, and has this beautiful long hair that is soooo silver it almost glows. When she has her flowing white dresses on, well, I suppose one would say she's as mesmerizing as an angel."

I looked at my friend skeptically. All this guru stuff is strange.

Alexis gathered her food wrappings and shoved them back into her bag. "Kali's great … but she brought on this 'second in command' recently who I haven't figured out yet. She seems helpful and nice enough, but, well…maybe she's not my cup of tea. Seems high strung and, I don't know, something's off. I'm not quite getting the 'peace vibe' from her," she emphasized with air quotes.

"Oooh, someone making trouble at Mercy…" I taunted.

"Uma Devi is her name. She's a tiny little thing—maybe five-two. The first noticeable thing about her though is her bright red hair. Not natural in the slightest; we're talking Flaming Cheetos-red, short, spiky hair. Talk about polar opposites, when you see the two gurus together," she laughed.

"And, that's what is 'off' about her?" I mimicked the exact same air quotes.

"No, no, no," she laughed. "There's something about her. It's a feeling I sense when talking to her. She's driven—seems to me to contradict that *finding inner peace* philosophy."

"So, in this group, you are at a level that you get to *speak* to the gurus directly? I mean, isn't that like talking to … God?"

"Oh, Libby … you are too funny. No! Everyone is treated equal and *yes*, we all talk freely amongst one another." She stopped in thought for a second. "Well, I suppose Kali is less attainable than all the others. You would have to make an appointment to get a direct audience with her. She's one busy lady—you know, she speaks at symposiums all over the world. Well-known among the celebrity types, too."

Another eye roll from me. It all sounds too woo-woo and strange. I have meditated with Alexis before—trying to fit it in my lifestyle to reap the supposed benefits. Nothing weird about that, but I do have a difficult time with the idea of following a guru … seems a little contrived for my liking. However, I love that Alexis and Bella share this because I see the good it has brought them; I'm not one to criticize something I don't fully understand. Tease them both a little—sure. But, I fully support them in their self-help exploration.

Shadow nudged me after waiting so patiently through lunch. Of course, she had been patient, because she caught a couple scraps that I had accidentally dropped. We threw away our wrappings, secured our lunch bags back into Alexis' car, and then took Shadow for a walk around the park before returning to work.

* * *

By the end of the day, I had completed six ninety-minute Ashiatsu sessions and I was beat. It was after seven in the evening when I saw my last client out. I cleaned up my therapy room, and ran around the Serenity Room wiping down surfaces again, refilling the tea selection, and emptying the trash cans. As I finished and walked into the office, a familiar friendly voice sounded. Shadow gave a friendly woof and ran over to greet him.

"Just finishing up, too?" Brian asked. "I was thinking about stopping across the street for some sushi on my way home. Wanna join?"

Oh, that sounded delicious and I was starving. "Sure, why not," I shrugged as I checked my phone to see if Greg had called. No missed calls or texts. I nodded, and then added, "Let me take Shadow home and feed her. Meet you over there at eight?"

"It's a plan! See you there." He turned to leave.

Shadow heard me mention dinner and was giving me the stare-down as I went to shut my computer off. *How does she do that?* This was the first dog I'd had who literally reads my mind and understands my words.

I masked up and walked into the sushi restaurant. Looking around, I saw Brian wave his arm from a corner booth; I walked over there and was greeted by a perky young guy who took my drink order. Sauvignon Blanc sounded best tonight. Only one glass and it's a short drive home. Realistically, I could even walk home from here.

"You had a long day, too, I see," Brian started.

"Yes, indeed. It was one session right after another today. I saw Mrs. Barney—the knee replacement."

He gave a huge smile. "Oh, yeah. Good, glad she took me up on the recommendation. She's done so well with her exercises, and she's healed well. It will do her a lot of good to combine massage with everything else she's doing."

After ordering a variety of sushi rolls, sashimi, and some hot and sour soup, we fell right into comfortable conversation. We discussed several different clients that we share and commented on the progression of each. We had a lot in common with work and I found it so easy to talk to Brian. He understood clinical conditions and it was natural talking about work without feeling as though you're boring the other person to death.

A couple of his stories had me laughing so hard. As therapists, we find ourselves in a variety of situations with clients that could be embarrassing—but, we're so used to it that we find the humor instead. We traded several recent 'tabletop confessions' and I had him laughing hysterically also.

"…and, what did you *do*?" he bellowed, wiping at his mouth with his napkin at the same time.

"Oh, I lit the candle, adjusted the sheet, and carried on seamlessly … that's what we do." I laughed as I lifted my wine glass for another sip.

"I think I'd have a hard time stifling a laugh. Have you ever laughed out loud?"

"No!" I said horrified.

"Not even a little snicker?"

I thought for a second and smiled. "Maybe a *little* snicker … hopefully she didn't notice!" I tried to take another piece of the caterpillar roll, but couldn't quite yet.

His laughter was contagious; he was holding his stomach as though it hurt, and it got me going again.

I looked up through watering eyes and saw that Diane and Kathleen had walked in and were seated a couple tables away. Suddenly, I felt awkward. After Kathleen's comment earlier, now she was observing us sharing a meal together, over drinks no less.

I set my napkin on the table, took a large gulp of water, and said, "Brian, this has been a great end to a busy day, but I think I'm going to have to call it a night."

"Oh, no! We were just getting started with the really good tales … don't go yet," he pleaded, reaching his hand across and setting it gently on top of mine.

Quickly, I jerked my hand back and checked my watch. It was now nine-thirty. I never eat this late … and even more rare, I barely stay up this late at night. "Unfortunately, I've got an early appointment tomorrow and I'd best get to bed."

We flagged down our waiter and each paid our share of the check. Walking out, we stopped and said hi to our colleagues. Kathleen gave me that wink and I waved her off. I did not enjoy her teasing. I was going to have to put that rumor to bed once and for all, tomorrow.

Once I got home, I discovered Greg had left me a voice message. He tried calling around eight. His message was simple: *Hey hon, trying to reach my sweetie … are you out there? It seems like it's been forever since we've had a nice long talk. Call me back if you get this in the next half hour or so. Otherwise, I'll try again tomorrow.*

My heart fluttered and suddenly I felt so guilty enjoying a nice dinner with another man.

CHAPTER THREE

Bella startled me when I finished listening to Greg's message.

"Oh! Didn't know you were there." She must have seen the distraught look to my face.

"What's wrong, Libby? Who was that?" she asked me.

"It was Greg." I was still considering calling him back.

"Awwwww, you miss him, don't you? It's been forever since I've seen him around here."

"He's working in New Mexico this week. Yes, it's been too long." I set my phone down, then changed the subject. "Hey, how are you doing? This morning you were upset. Feel like talking about it now? I don't want to pry, but you know that you can talk to me anytime, right?"

"I'm sorry, I didn't mean to shut you out earlier. Want some tea?"

"Sure, let's sit down with a nice cuppa—that fixes everything," I agreed.

Bella, Shadow, and I curled up on the large plush sofas. I asked her about Love & Mercy and how she was enjoying the fellowship. Her face lit up as she finally told me all about the last retreat she'd gone to and the people she had met. Jill Walsh was from California—she compared her to the typical surfer girl, with sun bleached hair and a deep bronzed tan. She said she was sweet and shy when they first met. She hadn't really opened up to anyone in the group, except for Bella. They were taking some of the self-help courses offered at Mercy—the current session they were completing was a women's course in confidence. She told me that both of them found it enlightening and they planned to sign up for the entire curriculum that would help them achieve the silver level badge.

"I didn't realize they have *levels*," I interrupted. "Are these free classes they offer?"

"Oh, no. Definitely not free … but I'm willing to invest in myself and they offer a variety of ways where we can work off our course fees."

I didn't exactly like the sound of that, but I also didn't want to shut her down entirely either. So, I encouraged her to continue telling me all about the course and the people involved. Eventually, she got to the part that had upset her earlier. This week, her friend Jill, started gushing over the older guy in their meditation session—his name was Joseph Banter. Lexi had filled me in, he was a media mogul; super wealthy, and according to Bella, a complete narcissist who didn't care at all about anyone but himself. He'd been with the group for about a month now and somehow was already 'in' with the gurus. Bella and several other members couldn't understand how—he barely followed the rules and everyone could see he was a 'cocky SOB'. No one could figure out why he had stuck around either. He scoffed at the ideology, snickered through meditation, flirted with every woman there … he was a joke. Apparently, Jill didn't appreciate Bella's opinion about Joseph and they got into an argument over that. Bella felt that he was manipulating her friend and she was blindly following.

"Ah, that makes more sense now. You care about what happens to your friend." I reached out for her hand and gave it a little squeeze. "You said something earlier about her wanting to quit the group?"

"Yeah. She's seriously considering it! But, a week or so ago, she was saying the exact opposite and going on about how helpful Mercy has been, and she was so grateful for all the friends she's made there, and how much more confident she was feeling. I'm not sure what changed." She shook her head slowly, then took a sip of tea, before looking over at me again. "I don't trust Joseph," she said emphatically.

"You mentioned he's older than her … like, by how much?"

"Oh God, I think he could be her *father*! Maybe early forties?" she rolled her eyes in disgust.

"And she's twenty-one?"

She nodded.

"Yeah, twenty-plus years older is quite a gap. Doesn't mean it couldn't work, but I guess I see your concern."

"Well, I'm not worried about the age gap. I'm worried that he's a narcissistic A-hole! Sorry." She looked over sheepishly.

"It's okay … get it all out!" I laughed. "Have you met

this guy? Do you think he has some control over her?" I tried carefully to broach the subject without her shutting down.

She shrugged. "I'm only going by what she's said about him."

"Okay. Well, I don't think there'll be anything you can do about Jill. She's her own woman and can see who she wants. The more you try to convince her otherwise, the more she'll resent you and stop listening altogether. My advice—stay close, and keep your lips sealed. Be there for her, but don't criticize. If Joseph is truly as bad as you think he is, she'll see it, too. Eventually. That's why staying close is important—so she always knows you are there for her. Continue taking the courses with her, and hopefully, they'll also help open her eyes."

"Thanks, Libby. I suppose you are right." She stood up and took her mug to the kitchen sink. "I've gotta hit it—way tired now!"

I sat there for a few more minutes contemplating the last several hours. It was too late to call Greg back now. *I'll call in the morning—I really need to hear his voice.* Then, Brian's smile entered my consciousness. He was a really nice friend to hang out with—funny, and we could talk for hours. I really liked having a work buddy now. Then, I thought about Kathleen. *Was I getting too close to Brian?*

* * *

By the time Shadow and I returned from our run the next morning, Bella was blending our favorite smoothie. Frozen avocado, blueberries, cherries, bone-broth protein, and raw fiber powder.

"Are you at the front desk this morning?" I asked her as I breezed by, grabbing my smoothie before heading to the shower.

"My shift starts at 1 p.m."

"Oh, then you're up super early!"

"I'm picking up some additional shifts at Healing Solutions." She saw the question form in my eyes as I poured kibble into Shadow's bowl. "I'm saving up for the next round of courses at Mercy. They're not cheap."

I nodded, and then headed off for my shower.

As the water cascaded down, I found myself wondering how Bella was managing the Mercy courses on top of completing her EMT certification. *And, just how much were these courses?* I was nearly finished rinsing off when I could hear my phone ringing in the distance. Shutting off the water and grabbing my towel, I hurried to my bedside where my phone was charging.

"Hey, handsome!" I answered, feeling the flutter I always got. "Sorry I missed you last night."

"Ah, that's the voice I was longing to hear," Greg purred. "Must have been a long day yesterday?"

"That's an understatement. But here we are … when are you coming home?"

"Not soon enough." His voice trailed off; he was sad. "They need me for a couple more weeks."

My heart dropped. I had hoped we'd be able to sneak in a couple days together within this week. "Ah well. That's not good, but I suppose it means they're thrilled with your forest restoration work. That's a positive thing, right?"

"I guess. I'd rather hold my beautiful girlfriend instead."

"I'm sure it won't be much longer." The disappointment dripped from our words. There was nothing that made this situation better, but both of our careers were important, too, I supposed.

We managed to get out of our funk and spent the next thirty minutes filling each other in on all the happenings. Despite the good conversation, I couldn't help but feel the distance. I had the distinct feeling that we were drifting apart and it made my heart hurt. The less-frequent conversations were becoming strained, too routine, and less exciting. It'd been six months since we first met. *Had I ever had a relationship last that long?* I felt the familiar pang in my heart that filtered down through to my gut. Sadness. *Why am I so horrible at this?*

CHAPTER FOUR

Alexis was behind the front counter when I got to work. Shadow ran around and gave her friend a nice slobbery kiss.

"Ah, now I understand," I grinned. Her inquisitive look prompted me to continue. "Bella said she wasn't here until the afternoon. I was wondering who was covering the front desk."

She laughed. "Yes, I volunteered. I didn't have any appointments this morning and I can do my computer work from this one."

"So, Bella talked to you about working other jobs?"

She nodded. "She's motivated to take more courses at Mercy. I think they're helping her."

"But, we hired her full-time for *our business*. Don't you

think we should discuss the ramifications of her absence being filled by one of the *partners*?" As I asked the question, I realized how irritated I actually was.

"Libby, you don't like her participation at Mercy, do you?"

"I don't want to make this about Mercy necessarily. That's not fair. My point is that *you* are sitting behind the front desk while Bella is next door working an additional job. She's supposed to be *here*." I pointed to the seat Alexis was occupying.

"Point taken." We both looked up to see a client walking up to the door. "Let's discuss this later in private."

We both smiled wide as the door opened. "Good morning, Ms. Wright!" we both chimed, in unison. Shadow also came around to greet our client. After our greetings, Shadow and I made our way back to the office as my phone started to ring.

"Hello, Mother," I answered, trying to quash the earlier irritation from my voice. "How's the neighborhood gang doing?" A month earlier, my mother and her neighbor started up the Neighborhood Watch group. There was a drug gang doing business in their senior community—including some suspicious antics they pulled on my mother. Shadow and I were not happy about that.

"Good morning, Libby! Uh, it's been boring lately. No random wandering people through our communities as of late," she sighed. "I was calling to see if you'd like to come over for dinner later?"

"That sounds great. Just us? Or will Jordan and the family be joining?" I hadn't seen my sister recently.

"It'll be the whole family. I've got a crock pot going—some recipe Dottie gave me. Crack Chicken, or something like that."

"Excellent! Count me in." After hanging up, I was still wondering what Crack Chicken was. No matter, Mom's cooking was always the best.

* * *

After another long day at the spa, I pulled up at my mother's home several miles away about six o'clock. Shadow leapt from the backseat when I opened the door. Jordan's kids were playing in the front and Shadow was eager to join them. The kids squealed in delight as she squirmed around them and demanded attention. I left them to play in the grass of the fenced front yard, while I found Jordan and our mother in the kitchen already pouring some wine.

Jordan immediately stated, "Don't worry, Libby. The kids are staying the night at Mom's and I'll only have one glass anyway." She pointed to the wine, as though I frequently lectured her about such concerns.

I shrugged, not understanding why she started off so defensively. I approached her and gave her a hug. "So nice to see you. It's been a while." Then, I came up behind my mom at the crock pot and reached around from behind, giving her a hug, too. "Oh, yummm, smells scrumptious!"

She turned around and gave me a peck on the cheek. "I'm so happy you both are here tonight! It *has* been a while since we've all been together." She handed me a glass of wine and then lifted her own. "To the Madsen women!"

"Cheers!" Both Jordan and I laughed after we had cheered in unison.

My mom set her glass on the counter. Quite animatedly, she placed her hand on a jutted-out hip. "How's *Greg* doing?" she teased.

"Yeah, how's that handsome boyfriend of yours?"

Jordan asked.

I wasn't expecting the subject so soon and hadn't prepared my reaction. They both detected as much from my expression of sadness.

"What's wrong, sweetie?" Mom reached out a hand to my shoulder. "Here, sit ... let's all sit."

"Greg is fine. No worries." I tried to blow past the subject.

"Sis, you don't fool us! Spit it out…"

I lifted my glass to take a sip. "He's working out of state—that's all. We haven't seen each other since the Utah vacation."

"Aww. You miss him!" my mom lifted her hands to her mouth. "How cute!"

Yeah, how cute.

"I've been busy at the spa. You know, with the phys…"

"Tell us about what he's doing out of state. Where?" Jordan interrupted.

"He's in New Mexico doing restoration work. The departments often share forest ranger teams and this time his team was commissioned out to New Mexico."

"Why so sad, hon?" my mom asked.

"I'm not …" She gave the look like 'don't try and fool me'. "Okay, I am a little sad. I want this relationship to work."

"Why can't it?" Jordan asked.

Starting to feel defeated, or ambushed, in this conversation, I sighed. "It can. I'm starting to feel that perhaps the relationship has already run its course. Long distance…"

"You're only two hours away!" my mom inserted.

"…is *difficult*," I finished pointedly.

Saved by bell, the timer sounded and Mom scooted over to the oven. "Jordan, get the kids washed up for dinner. We'll set them up at the table right here. The three of us will eat in the dining room."

The noise level was intense as four screeching children ran through the house and into the bathroom. I could hear Jordan admonish one of her boys with "Chase, stop!" Then, instructing, "with soap, please…" presumably to the whole clan. Shadow found herself at my mom's feet, waiting for her to drop something yummy.

"C'mon, Shadow. Out of the kitchen," I prodded her out with one of her cookies, which she has in her own cookie jar in grandma's kitchen. Once in the living room, I motioned *sit* with my hands and gave the verbal command. She tried her hardest to stay still, but it took several seconds for her bottom to actually hit the floor. "Down." I signaled for her to lay down. "Good girl!" I gave her the cookie and told her to stay. Pride was flowing through me when I walked out of the room and she actually followed her command. I waited for several moments to be sure she stayed, then I walked back to her and gave her a bully stick, which was sure to keep her busy while we ate our dinner.

The kids were already digging into their bowls of the creamy chicken stew. It was the first time since we'd arrived that I wasn't hearing their voices. This Crack Chicken *must* work miracles.

I grabbed a bowl as instructed, along with a piece of the toasted garlic bread, and found my seat at the dining room table. Jordan's comment as I sat caught my attention.

"You know of Love & Mercy?" I had no idea.

"Oh yeah. After Pat left, I was floundering. I have found their self-help courses to be a lifesaver." She blew on the hot spoonful of stew before putting it in her mouth.

"Bella's been doing the same. But, I never knew much about them before her ... well, and Lexi. She's one of their meditation instructors so she's been leading sessions for a while now. Lex doesn't talk much about the place though—I didn't know until recently that they have self-help courses."

"How's Bella affording that place?" Jordan's eyebrows lifted. "It's horribly expensive."

"Oh yeah? Like, how expensive?"

"Thousands *per course*."

I nearly dropped my spoon. *How is Bella affording that?* "Wow, had no idea. I know she's picking up more jobs to save up, but I also know she's paying for her EMT courses, too." I shrugged. "Guess she's figuring it all out. You haven't seen her around the Mesa center?"

Jordan chuckled. "Nooo, it's *huge*. And, I'm already at the gold level so we wouldn't be in the same courses." There was an arrogant tone I chose to ignore.

"What do these *levels* signify anyway?"

"Oh, there's a whole path to enlightenment!" She got giddy with excitement as she spent the next half hour telling us all about this spiritual path. We let her educate us as we enjoyed the scrumptious chicken stew. I'd have to get the recipe—guess it was aptly named, this could be super addictive.

Later that night, as I was lying in bed ruminating on the day's events, I couldn't believe that my sister was also involved in this organization, Love & Mercy. *Was I the only one who wasn't?* Lexi, Bella, and now Jordan. And, as my sister explained, the amount of money you'd spend before reaching the Blue Diamond, or 'enlightenment' level was insane. *And, how many levels did she say there were?* I'm not sure she actually said, but it sounded like it was more than ten. I think I figured out you'd spend hundreds of thousands to reach the end of their program. But that wasn't the only thing bothering me. The way Jordan explained it, that was on top of annual fees, retreats (which were not free to members), and repeating courses if you happened to fail. Plus, it sounded like there were several self-help programs—the one Jordan and Bella were doing was just the beginning. *What prevents the organization from keeping you at a certain level for years—raking in the moola the entire time?*

Finally, I put Love & Mercy out of my head and fell asleep. Around midnight.

CHAPTER FIVE

I dragged myself through my morning routine, completely kicking myself for obsessing and preventing sleep because of this spiritual group infiltrating my family. When I made it to the kitchen, I noticed that coffee was brewed and Bella had already left. It wasn't even six-thirty yet.

Shadow and I took a break from our long run and decided that walking to work this morning would count as our workout.

Brian was leaning over into the backseat of his car for something as we passed by. Shadow barked and got a smile out of the gentle healer. "Hey, Shadow ... hey, Libby!" He pulled out his backpack, closed the door, put on his mask, and walked into the building with us. "Looks like we're going to have a meditation session here tonight. I've been telling all my clients."

I was confused. *Why hadn't I heard about this? Was Lexi leading the session?* I asked Brian and he indicated there had been flyers up in the break room all week. *Really?* I hadn't noticed.

"Are you going to join us?" he asked excitedly.

"I'll think about it." I turned to indicate I was headed to my office. "Have a great day, Brian!"

Alexis was at her desk and on the phone when I walked through the door. When she got off, she got up and grabbed her mug. "Wanna cuppa?" she offered.

"Sure. A pick-me-up, please. Maybe not one of the herbals…" I smiled.

"Ah, rough night?" she nudged.

I laughed. "Well, it was a night with Mom, Jordan, and the kids … maybe that's what wore me out?"

She left the room to get our tea and I unloaded my lunch into our private office mini-fridge. As I did so, I privately acknowledged that I'd always kept my food with the other employees in our break room. *Was I avoiding running into Brian so often?* No—I'm not changing my routine because of some stupid rumor that may, or may not, be going around the office. I closed the mini-fridge and headed to the lunch room instead.

Bella was at the coffee machine when I walked in.

"Thanks for the coffee this morning!"

She turned around. "Of course. Looks like you need more?" She held up a mug she'd washed out.

"I'm going to try some black tea. We'll see … I might be back." I said, rolling my eyes. "Oh, hey … I had dinner with my sister last night and she says she's taking a gold-level course at the Mesa center." It rolled off my tongue as though I was so knowledgeable.

Bella perked up. "Really? That's great! I've never run into her there, but I'll keep my eyes open. Well, gotta get back to the front desk."

That reminded me that I still needed to talk to Lexi about Bella's schedule. I put my lunch in the refrigerator and went back to my office.

Alexis was walking back in as I sat in my chair.

"Thank you, ma'am." I took the mug she handed to me. "Hey, listen … I'm sorry for being curt yesterday regarding Bella's schedule. That's your business with her and I didn't mean to question you."

She nodded slightly, and sighed. "You have a point though, Libs. I'll talk to her."

"I guess I'm confused, though. She's hourly—how does missing a shift here, to work next door, help her save money?"

"They pay way better apparently," she succinctly stated.

"Oh. Well, are we able to match? Maybe then she wouldn't have to pick up extra work elsewhere?"

"I'll take a look now that we are bringing in more business. I doubt it though. They're paying her double what we could pay her."

"Something doesn't seem right about that. How are they able to?"

"Physical therapy is huge business—"

I was frustrated. "She's going to ultimately leave us for them, isn't she?"

"Well, I can't say that … she's devoted to us and I don't think she'll leave us in a lurch. But, she does have to take care of herself."

"Yeah, I know. And, she's paying me rent now too … so, it's not like she's taking advantage *and* looking for more ways to earn." I remembered about Mercy. "Hey, I do have a different concern though."

"Okay…?"

"I was talking to Jordan last night, and she was telling me exactly how much these courses cost at Mercy. She's a member now too."

Her eyes lifted in curiosity. "She is? I had no idea…"

"Yep, gold level." I waited to see if that came as a surprise to her. Did my friend know all about these levels and the money involved?

"Hmmm."

"Lexi, you are a meditation instructor there. Are you paying for these self-help courses, too?"

She shook her head. "No, although, I've really started to consider their next women's health session."

"But, you know that each course cost *thousands* of dollars, right?"

Apparently, she didn't. That caught her off guard.

"So, you can lead meditation sessions there, but they don't require you to be a member … or pay for courses, or anything?"

"Yeah, apparently. I've been helping there since before the pandemic—of course, there were many weeks when they closed. But, yeah … I haven't been asked to pay for anything. I do volunteer my time leading sessions. I don't want to get paid for meditation sessions," she scoffed.

"Hmmm. Maybe that proves I'm wrong?"

"About what?"

"That they are after the money and brainwashing their members."

She laughed. "Brainwashing? Libby, it's a great organization. What's the problem?"

"There probably isn't one." I took a sip of my tea. "But, how will Bella pay thousands for these courses?"

"Sounds like that is for her to work out," she smiled gently. "Relax. Hey, I've got a session and I need to set up my room. It'll be okay—stop your worrying."

"Hey, you're holding a meditation session here tonight?"

"Yeah, you should join…" she said, as she left the room.

I couldn't help it; I pulled up Love & Mercy on the internet and started to do some research for myself.

CHAPTER SIX

That evening when I entered the Serenity Room, I was amazed at the transformation. I'd decided to show up and try meditation again … mostly, because I knew my friend was leading it.

Most of the furniture was moved aside along the walls, the lighting was dim and candles were glowing around the room. Lexi had set up a platform of sorts where she placed one of the oversized pillow chairs slightly above the rest of the group. Wearing a beige floral paisley tunic and long flowing linen pants, she looked regal from her perch. In her perfect posture, and with a softened facial expression, she nodded her head and lowered her eyes, signaling for me to take one of the cushions placed on the floor.

The room was nearly silent. No one spoke, even though

several people were still entering the building. There had to be at least fifteen people already seated, with face masks on. All the floor cushions, and the several folding chairs, were spread around the room with plenty of distance between, all facing toward Alexis.

I felt out of place and uncomfortable, but quietly sat on a white cushioned seat. Looking around, I noticed that everyone's eyes were already closed so I followed suit. My heart was thumping and I couldn't believe I had decided to join a group meditation session. *What was I thinking?* I peeked out to see if everyone was staring at me—so self-conscious. Nope, everyone's eyes were closed and presumably I was the only one whose voice was screaming inside my head to *get out*. At the very moment I'd made the decision that's exactly what I was going to do, my friend's comforting voice softly sounded. *Crap, I'm trapped.*

"Welcome friends. Let's all take a deep breath in … hold it for a count of four … then, slowly, let it out for four. Here we go…" she expertly led us through several breathing exercises. Before I knew it, after guiding us through what she called 'soul questions', she completed the thirty minutes of silence with a few sutras and a Namaste. When I finally opened my eyes, I was surprised how settled I felt. More amazing, I had forgotten about all the people in the room. It was impressive how Lexi could do that.

I slowly moved to standing, feeling slightly unsteady for a second. I looked across the room and made eye contact with the handsome redhead. Brian was moving in my direction.

He bowed in Namaste. "I'm happy to see that you made it here tonight. Wasn't that amazing?" he asked me; I nodded and smiled in agreement, not sure what to do or say. He glowed with … well, enlightenment. *Was that it? Had he been doing this for a long time? Wait, do I look enlightened now, too?* "The group from Mercy is amazing—I'll never regret going down this path."

"Wait, these are members from Mercy?" I asked.

"Yes, of course." He stared at me. "You're friends with Alexis; you didn't know that?"

"I guess I thought it was our staff and clients joining for the session here tonight. Honestly, I've been so busy lately, I didn't even really know about this until you told me earlier this morning."

He laughed. "Yeah, look over there…that's our guru, Kali Patel." Exactly as Lexi had described earlier. Brian also looked enamored by the stunning silver-haired woman with the delicate features. She was quietly talking with a man who was of equal height and equally enthralled with her as Brian was. "We're blessed to have her join us; she's usually jet-setting around the world delivering her divine messages."

I nearly broke out laughing, but quickly discovered that he was serious. He had placed this woman on a pedestal in his mind. Apparently, so did everyone else in the room, judging by the line waiting to speak to her.

"And, here … behind you. That's Uma Devi. She's *ah-maz-ing*—still new to the organization, but she has quickly been accepted for sure."

I turned slowly to look behind me; didn't want to be that obvious. Over near the tea station, she was talking to Bella. Yep, Lexi was correct—that was some *red* hair! I excused myself from Brian and decided to have Bella introduce me to the petite woman.

Walking right up to them, I exclaimed, "Bella, wasn't

that *ah-maz-ing?*" I accentuated like Brian had, trying to fit in. "Oh, I'm sorry … I interrupted."

"No, no. Please, I'm honored to introduce you to one of our gurus, Libby!" She turned to Uma, "Guru Devi, this is Libby Madsen. She is Alexis' business partner here at the spa. Libby, this is Guru Uma Devi."

Looking down several inches, I was mesmerized by her stunning emerald green eyes. Before she spoke, I couldn't help but notice the peace that emanated as she slowly put her palms together and bowed toward me.

"Namaste," she quietly said, and then gently looked up again, smiling. "So nice to meet you, Libby Madsen."

"Nice to meet you too, uh … Ms. Devi." I shifted my weight and wiped my sweaty palms along my leggings.

"Libby, I was telling my guru that you were asking me questions about the organization." Bella caught my questioning eyes. *Why would she talk about me to the guru?* "She reminded me that I could invite someone to the Mesa center anytime I'd like."

I couldn't move. Not having expected to come up with the excuse of the century, I was paralyzed in place. My eyes bored into Bella's trying to send the telepathic message to cease conversation.

"Yes, Libby … we would be honored for you to join us. Please consider." She touched my shoulder lightly and I swear electricity shot through me. "I need to touch base with a few others before I leave tonight, please excuse me."

"Uh, ok. Yes, I'll think about it," I called out to her as she walked away. Then, I turned to Bella. She smiled sweetly. I wanted to tell there was no way I was going to get involved, but the words wouldn't form.

"They have a lecture tomorrow night at the center, if

you're interested. It sounds cool—something related to discovering gratitude in difficult times." Her innocence was refreshing, and her optimism was contagious.

"How long are these lectures?"

"Starts at six-thirty and after a short meditation, maybe an hour tops?"

"I'm sure I have a ..."

She was already shaking her head. She knew my schedule better than I did. "Your last session ends at four-thirty; plenty of time." She smiled, touched my arm as she turned to depart. "I'll drive!"

* * *

After work the next day, I quickly stopped by my mom's house to pick up a casserole she had made for us. She was always doing generous things like that. And, honestly, if my weeks weren't filled in with a pot of soup or a new casserole from her, there were many nights I probably wouldn't eat. Sometimes I came home so exhausted that I literally forgot.

Bella and I enjoyed the pork carnitas enchilada casserole before we loaded up in her car for our evening's adventure.

"You're going to *love* this ... the people are great. The lectures are informative." She let out of a tiny squeal of excitement. "I'm so happy you agreed to come tonight!"

I didn't remember exactly *agreeing*, but true, I didn't protest and now, here we are. In my head, I was giving myself the pep talk that it would be nice to meet new people. I do love learning new topics and surely, it wouldn't hurt to learn to be more gracious. As we pulled into the parking lot of the enormous Love & Mercy center, I kept repeating: *You will be okay. You will be okay.*

I never knew the place existed here in Mesa. The building was two stories tall, a brown stone exterior, many windows—some stained-glass—and luscious shrubbery with tall trees all around. The path's lighting showcased a perfectly manicured lawn on either side. It was gorgeous. With the sun near fully set, the signage out front glowed pink from strategically placed lighting. *How had I missed this previously?* We pulled into the first parking spot we could find. All the spaces had filled up quickly.

We walked up the long sidewalk leading to the grand front entrance. Large stone pillars flanked a waterfall that towered above us. The amber lighting displayed a nice sized pond, filled with water lilies. Soft white lighted lotus flowers floated about. *They must have spent a fortune on this place.*

After we donned our masks, Bella opened the doors and we stepped into a great hall where people were gathered in small groups. A small woman handed us a tiny glass I would have recognized as a shot glass. Bella took one, so I did as well.

"Fresh ginger, turmeric, and orange juice. It's a digestive; they serve fresh juice and these healing/cleansing shots at all the centers. The best part is that it's *free*—you don't have to purchase juice here!" She was clearly thrilled with the amenity, not even considering that her course fees probably pay for a *lot* of juice. We pulled our masks down temporarily, took our shots, and set the little glasses on the designated tray.

I was replacing my mask on my face as I let my eyes roam around the extensive space. It was an interior designer's mecca. Lined with numerous tall bamboo trees, along with another water feature—a smaller fountain which filled a lazy river that snaked through the room, it was as if we had stepped into another world. In the middle, there was a large bronzed statue of Lord Ganesh and to his right, there was a beautifully adorned bridge. Apparently, you had to cross that bridge to get into the auditorium, I guessed. Off to the far left from the doors we had entered, there was a hallway, presumably to other rooms—maybe the classrooms where Bella took her courses, I thought. To my right, at the far end, maybe fifty yards away, there was a grand staircase that led to the upper level.

As I was admiring the stunning décor, I found myself staring at the lovely guru, Kali Patel, seemingly floating down the expansive staircase. Her long silver locks floated as effortlessly as the chiffon train of her gorgeous colorful sari. When her bare feet grounded to earth at the bottom of the staircase, she walked purposefully through the room, her eyes squarely on the wooden bridge. It was as though everyone knew what to do. As she crossed the bridge, everyone fell in behind her—crossing the bridge together, dutifully following their leader.

I trailed behind Bella into the grand auditorium, nervously looking about as though I was about to be ... *What? Why was I so anxious? What exactly did I think was going to occur?* We found seats several rows from the front at center stage. I looked around and caught sight of my sister Jordan sitting next to a lovely looking older gentleman, quite the silver fox. They were clear on the other side of the auditorium behind me. She didn't see me, but I'd try to catch up with her later; she appeared to be in deep quiet conversation and there was no way I was getting up now. I'd be the center of attention and would surely fall, or make a loud sound that would break the hushed quietness in the room. No, I decided to stay put. As I continued to survey my surroundings, I noticed that this place could probably hold tens of thousands. It was like stadium seating, high into the rafters. Tonight, however, I guessed there were about fifty to seventy-five people attending. I'm sure the pandemic limited them from the crowds they were used to.

Movement to my left had me turn to look. I saw the other cute guru with the spiky red hair that I'd talked to the night before. With her palms together in front of her heart, she slowly glided toward the center stage where Kali had already found her place, cross-legged on a large round floor cushion. When Uma arrived at her seat, she bowed slightly to Kali with her hands still at her heart. Kali bowed to her, then Uma crossed her legs and effortlessly squatted into the same cross-legged position on the floor. She made it look so easy. *Yep, I need to try that at home*—wondering if my legs were that strong and flexible.

"Welcome, my lovelies!" Kali's soft voice echoed throughout the chamber. "Let's take a moment to give our gratitude. Please close your eyes."

I did as instructed and felt much calmer about it than I did last night in the smaller group setting. Was it the size of this place? It didn't feel as intimate, but maybe I was getting the hang of this after all.

Following the guru's lead, repeating silently in my head the soul questions, and visualizing the gratitude messaging she put forth, I settled down. So relaxed and calm for twenty minutes or so. We opened our eyes when instructed; everything in the room appeared to me more defined. My vision was crisper, like cobwebs were dusted away. I settled in and found myself riveted as the gurus took turns delivering a well-organized and informative lecture about gratitude. The time sped by.

Bella looked over, "Libby, we can get up now." She nudged a bit. I shook my head slightly and turned to her smiling.

"I've never been so relaxed before. Can we just sit here for a few more seconds?"

She laughed. "As long as you'd like."

Once I saw that most people had cleared the room, I leaned over to grab my purse off the floor. "Okay. Can we go get some more juice?" I smiled.

"Sure!"

We headed out to the great hall of bamboo, crossed the bridge, and headed over to the fresh juice station. There was a menu detailing their juice selections. Everything from the Green Goddess (kale, spinach, apple, ginger, and lemon) to Uma's Favorite (carrot, beet, red pepper, orange, ginger, and lemon). I chuckled, looking at the picture—as red as her hair; aptly named for sure. Bella and I chose cleansing green juices before setting out to find my sister.

As soon as we stepped away from the juice bar, Kali walked right up to us. I suddenly felt awkward, as though I was meeting a well-known celebrity. My palms were clammy and mouth dry, even though I'd just taken a sip of my green drink.

"Bella!" Kali leaned over and kissed her on one cheek, then the other. "Introduce me to your friend, love," Kali stated in her ethereal soft-as-a-whisper voice.

"Kali, this is Libby..." she grabbed my hand as she turned to me, "Libby, this is my guru, Kali Patel."

In my amateurish manner, after she kissed one cheek, I nearly kissed her straight on the lips as she moved to kiss the other cheek. Both of my cheeks flamed red now, as I coyishly apologized for my gaffe. She moved on without missing a beat.

"It's so lovely to meet you, Libby. I understand you took in this lovely girl recently. We adore Bella here." She stared admiringly at Bella, then back to me.

"Yes, yes, that's correct. I have been honored to help her out. She certainly didn't deserve … well, let's say I think she's in a much better place now," I said, as I looked around the beautiful room. "It's not all me, you know. It takes a village." Yes, I was rambling on while I was sure the guru had better things to do.

Kali turned to my friend. "Bella, you know you can bring a 'plus one' to our upcoming retreat. Bring Libby!"

Bella and I stared at one another briefly. My mind raced; what kind of excuse do you give a guru? Ok, she's not exactly a medium so she can't read my mind, but do you lie to a guru? Won't karma come back in spades? *Ugh, I do not want to go on retreat.*

"Oh, well … uh, you know. I've got a puppy at home. Can't leave her. My very large puppy—black Lab. I'm truly sorry, but I don't see how I could…" I was definitely rambling uncomfortably, and hoping that 'large dog' would definitely work.

Her face glowed in the wake of her smile. "Not a problem. You have your own space at our retreat. Please bring your puppy. She's more than welcome," she stated, then turned her head as another couple was approaching. "Think about it."

I had the distinct feeling that no one had ever rejected this woman. She had that sort of presence. As she walked away, I called after her, "Thank you! I'll think about it."

"See you there!" she teased, looking back over her shoulder and winking.

CHAPTER SEVEN

The next day began quietly enough, but by the end of the day, I'd call it chaotic. First, we had to deal with a medical emergency with one of our clients. Poor lady. Not long after the paramedics had left and things settled down, Bella came running back to the office. She needed to leave urgently. I agreed to clean up and shut down the front desk for her.

Once everyone had left the building, I took several moments in the relaxation area to simply catch my breath. Shadow curled up next to me on the sofa and I rested my head back against the cushion. Only a few minutes later, Shadow stirred. There was a sound. She barked and went to investigate. *I thought we were alone.* Then, I heard his voice and Shadow's tail whipping the air.

"What are you still doing here?" I asked Brian.

"Just came back for my wallet—left it in the locker. I saw lights on over here and thought I'd check to be sure they weren't left on accidentally. And, well … I found you here. Hey, I was meaning to text you earlier … wanna join me for a hike in the morning?"

"Sure, sounds fun! Seven? Meet me at the house?" Even as I said it, I felt a pang for Greg.

"Yep, see you at seven. Have a great evening. And, hey, get out of here—you don't live in the spa, you know."

I laughed and watched him walk out. He was a good friend. *Just* a friend.

My phone rang as I was going around turning off lights.

"Bella—are you…"

I didn't finish before she cut me off, voice tight and clearly crying. "Libby. Jill is gone!"

"What do you mean … *gone*?"

"Earlier she called me, super upset. I'm at her apartment and *everything* is gone. I was supposed to pick her up for our class at the center. She's moved out! How can that be?"

"Okay, slow down. I'm getting ready to leave the spa. Let's meet at home so you can tell me everything."

"I'm supposed to go to class!"

"Do you feel well enough? You sound awfully upset. Maybe tonight's not the best night to go?"

She paused for a very long moment and I held my phone up to see if we had lost connection. We were still connected. "Bella?"

She choked out, "Sorry. I don't know what to do."

"For now, get home. Then we'll figure out what's next. Okay?"

She gave a stifled 'uh, huh' and hung up.

I couldn't imagine someone could actually move out of an apartment that fast. But, I don't know the girl at all— maybe she's a minimalist and has few possessions? Maybe she intended to move all along and Bella wasn't in the know about her plans? There were so many possibilities that I decided not to become concerned until I learned more of the story.

"C'mon Shadow, let's go!" We walked through the frosted glass doors, to the front desk where I shut off the remaining lights and we locked the doors.

Bella beat us home; Jill must not live too far away. I set down all my stuff and joined her on the sofa where I put my arms around her.

"You okay, kiddo?" I softly spoke.

She sniffled. Slowly, she turned toward me. "Jill is in trouble, Libby. We've got to help her."

"What makes you think this? What kind of trouble?"

"Last night she shared with me that she and Joseph have gotten close. They were on a date and he convinced her to come back to his place. When they got there, several members from the center were there. She thought that was strange and questioned why they were in his home while they had been out on a date."

"That's a very good question. And, wait, is this the Silicon Valley guy?"

She nodded her head.

"And, he lives here in Arizona, too? I guess I thought he only attended some courses and maybe retreats."

"From what she told me, he has homes all over. Yes, I'm pretty sure he mostly spends his time in California, but since the company has required him to take courses from the center, he's been staying at his Paradise Valley home. I guess. I don't really know for sure."

"Oh, okay. So, what happened next?"

"She got cagey and wouldn't spell it out for me exactly, but it sounded as though it was one of *those* parties," she emphasized, giving me that knowing look.

I had no idea what people do at parties. Even when I was younger, I was playing outdoors way more than I was drinking or whatever youth do at parties. But, I urged her to continue. When she did, she started sweating and wiping her palms on her jeans.

"Jill is certain that Joseph is involved in … oh, I don't exactly know … *something* not legal. She overheard something and said she'd tell me the specifics later; she couldn't talk long. She did hurriedly say that there were underage girls there. She was certain there were drugs, but after overhearing something that shook her up pretty badly, she said she had quietly ordered an Uber and then snuck out while they were distracted."

"Wow. So, these spiritual people are also partiers!" Then, I realized that wasn't supportive of my friend, so I went back to a more serious tone. "Okay, now, do you think that he brought Jill back to his place thinking that she wanted to get involved … doing, what, drugs and such?" I was confused why she was so afraid. Many teens and young twenties are partying like this—but, what had spooked Jill?

"Libby, I have no idea. But, I know one thing—this is *not* what Mercy is about. Kali would be appalled. Also, I got the feeling that Jill saw or heard much more than she relayed to me. I'm shocked by what she did tell me. Well, maybe with Joseph it's not shocking—seems the type—maybe that's to be expected, but *the others*? And, I'm wondering who exactly was there. Jill was certainly upset, so was it someone higher up in the organization? Not sure, but there is something that's not right here."

"So, what does this have to do with Jill moving out? Do you think she went back to California?"

She hung her head. "I'm afraid that Jill may have gone to confront someone … or, maybe threatened to tell Kali? I'm not sure. But, one thing I do know … she loved it here, and also, best I know, she had no intention of moving away. Something is very wrong."

I got up from the sofa. "Want a cup of chamomile?"

She nodded.

As I heated the kettle, I got to thinking back to the lecture we were at last night. I didn't remember seeing Joseph there. I don't know what Jill looks like, but presumed she also wasn't there. By eight o'clock the event was over.

"Hey, Bells, did Jill indicate what time it was when they got back to Joseph's place?"

She got up and walked up to the breakfast bar and sat on a stool facing me. "I'm not sure she did, but it had to have been late. They had dinner and saw a movie before that."

"Hmm. Yeah, makes sense. How is it that you think I could help?"

Her demeanor changed from worried to eager. "Wellll…" she started, and I knew she was preparing to sell me on something. My eyes narrowed, but encouraged her to continue. "Have you been thinking about Kali's invitation?"

My eyes lifted and I laughed. "Oh! So, now you want me to join in on this organization's shenanigans? Isn't that what you were worried about not two seconds ago?"

"It's not like that, Libby! No, no, no … that is absolutely

not what Love & Mercy is about. I swear to you."

"How does my attending the annual retreat locate Jill, who probably moved back to her parents in California?"

She hung her head as she sighed loudly. She slowly looked up. "Jill paid to go on this retreat—it's expensive, so I can't imagine she'd miss it. *If* she's there, maybe you can befriend her, and get more out of her than I was able. You are just so good at that kind of thing."

"Good at what?"

"Getting people to open up to you! Look what you've done for me."

I hadn't thought of it that way, but this was different and I really couldn't imagine spending four days trying to be on my best behavior and pretending I'm into what they're preaching. But, I would be lying to myself if I didn't acknowledge that deep down I was extremely curious. *Had Jill overheard something that could bring down this giant institution?*

"When is this retreat?"

She smiled hugely, jumped up and came around the counter with a hug. "It's week after next."

"Wow, that soon? October sixteenth?"

"Um, whatever the Thursday through Tuesday is … the fifteenth, I think, is when we check in?"

"Okay. Count me in. But, don't expect that I'm going to come home all 'Namaste' and stuff! And, now, you really owe me." I stopped short. "Were they serious I could bring Shadow?"

"Yeah, of course."

That seemed over-the-top—I suppose they were really interested in recruiting me. Well, good luck to them, I smiled to myself.

CHAPTER EIGHT

A couple weeks later, The Love & Mercy van picked us up at the pre-dawn hour of four o'clock. Once I stashed my bag in the back as they advised, I put on my face mask and then led Shadow to the passenger door. Bella was right behind us. There, they took our temperature before allowing us to board. I wondered when I'd finally get used to the new protocols all businesses had to institute. We climbed in once we passed that test. There were two other passengers already on board and we were told we'd pick up two more on our way out of town. The twelve-passenger van was at half its capacity once we were on I-10 headed east, with our ultimate destination in Southern Arizona, outside of the cute town of Patagonia.

I hadn't spent a whole lot of time in Southern Arizona,

but I had been to Patagonia Lake before. It was a beautiful place to camp and I remember that I had found the tiny town eclectic and interesting, but couldn't remember much more about it. The Love & Mercy compound was about seven miles west of town. I had read that they owned a huge swath of land—something like four hundred acres, which was astounding.

The lady with dark hair and deep brown eyes in the seat two rows behind us introduced herself. Her Spanish accent was thick.

"Hola, I am Katerina Sanchez. Most people call me Katie. This is my newfound friend, Danny. Danny McCall. Have you been members long?" she sweetly asked.

"Oh. Well, Bella is the *member* ... I'm her guest for the weekend retreat. I'm Libby, this is my faithful pup, Shadow." I turned to look at Bella, "And, this is my friend, Bella." They all put their palms together and bowed a Namaste to one another. Awkwardly, I belatedly followed suit. *I've got to remember their etiquette—er, ritual? Whatever.*

"I have come to all of their retreats. You will *love* this place. It's amazing!" she gushed. Katerina remembered seeing Bella around the center this week, but they'd never officially met. She told us she'd traveled from the center in New York for this retreat and to visit the one-of-its-kind Mesa center. She seemed sweet; Danny was an older gentleman, timid and quiet. My first impression was that he was of German descent—or some European heritage. However, he barely spoke so it was hard to say. It would be nice to walk into the place having met a few more members so I felt good about that. Still, I was nervous, and equally curious about the whole thing. I found my mind wandering. *Why did I agree to do this?* Then, of course, my thoughts went straight to Greg. I really missed him and we'd hardly talked over the last couple weeks while I was getting ready for this retreat. *Had I told him about it?* I couldn't remember off hand. The rest of our three-hour journey was quiet as each of us were lost in our own thoughts, or were busy scanning our devices. Shadow was curled up at my feet snoring away.

As we rounded the last turn and approached a huge gate with a copper patina, along with a beautiful Spanish style gatehouse, my stomach began to flutter. Was it excitement? Or, nerves? I wasn't sure yet. The van driver rolled up to the gatehouse and a sizable security guard stepped out, showcasing his enormous muscles in a tight black t-shirt and fitted black slacks. They spoke a few words, then the driver turned back to us and asked for us to step out of the van. All cell phones, tablets, computers, and cameras were to be left securely with the guard.

What? I turned to Bella with wide eyes, silently questioning the instruction we were given. She shrugged and pulled out her phone. Since I hadn't been on my device earlier, no one in the van knew whether I had brought one. As I gathered my belongings, and everyone else was busy doing the same, I slyly turned my phone off and tucked it into the obscure pouch inside of Shadow's bra. I grabbed my oversized tote bag, told Shadow to stay, and I climbed out of the van.

The enormous security man took her iPhone and then asked Katie to open her purse and he visually scanned it. I could see that he didn't have her empty it out—thank goodness. Danny was next, then Bella, and finally the guard scrutinized my bag.

"Phone, please," he demanded.

"I didn't bring one. Was told not to." I gave him a grin, as though *I* was the only one who *actually* followed the rules.

His piercing gaze had me nervous that he wasn't buying my story. He motioned again for me to open my bag. I complied. He harrumphed after rummaging around in my private stuff, giving it an extra once-over, but ultimately letting me go when he realized that I didn't have any electronic equipment in my purse.

"Everyone back on board!"

I was shaking slightly. Thank goodness he didn't ask about Shadow and have her come out for inspection too.

We moved slowly through the gate; I looked through the window, watching the guard glower toward our group as he gradually disappeared back into his station.

I turned to Bella and whispered, "Don't you wonder what he's going to do with those phones?"

She gave me a questioning look, but shrugged and shook her head, mouthing 'no.' I wasn't sure when I turned so cynical, or when everyone else became so trusting, but the vibes I got back there with Mr. Muscle were not good. *Why does a religious organization need all this security? What are they afraid of if people did take their phones in?* I was relieved that Bella hadn't noticed how I'd stashed mine and never questioned that I had left it at home.

We pulled up to the grand entrance. If I thought the Mesa center was over-the-top, this place was beyond compare. Similar features in many ways—the bronzed statues of Ganesh, Lakshmi, and Shiva; expansive water features; in fact, I believe all the elements were represented: water, fire, air, and earth. It was stunning.

After unloading our bags for us, the driver bowed and said goodbye. We followed the sidewalk flanked by flaming three-foot glass walls. The fire element was impressive as we approached glass doors with the Love & Mercy lotus flower logo etched on them. Two staffers opened the doors for us, with trays in their hands, offering us the 'wellness shot of the day'. It was a layered purple, red, and orange liquid in a small shot glass. My guess was this was Uma's Favorite. We accepted them and downed the sweet swallow of wellness. Now, it was time to check in at the front desk.

All guests would have their own casitas. Most of them were two-person dwellings, but I learned there were several that accommodated families. As the nice lady read off a ton of instructions to us, I realized for the first time that this was a *silent* retreat. I turned to my friend questioningly. *I'm going to kill Bella.* The staffer explained today's schedule: settle in the casita, a tour of the grounds, lunch with Uma, afternoon yoga, dinner, and Satsang with Kali. After Satsang, we all must observe silence until the final meditation on the last full day of retreat. All I focused on was 'settle in the casita,' oh, and maybe 'tour of the grounds.' The rest sounded like too much—we just got here, for heaven's sake.

Shadow was squirming at my feet. I kept patting her head letting her know it was okay. Soon, we were led outside where a lineup of golf carts awaited to transport guests. We hopped onto one.

"Welcome, my friends. My name is Badri and I'm here to serve you during retreat. Would this be your first time with us?" We saw his large smile looking at us in the rearview mirror. We both nodded in unison, mesmerized by the trill in his Indian accent. "Oh, you are in for a treat! You'll notice in the back there are several large containers of water. I will bring you fresh ones each day. We encourage you to hydrate well, after all, you are in the desert. As you know, this is a health retreat and we only serve up the healthiest ingredients for all our meals. This also includes fresh spring water. All food is grown right here on our property, and yes, we have a spring where the water comes from too. You will learn more on the tour."

We smiled and acknowledged how fancy everything was as we passed multiple dwellings we felt had to be where the uppity-ups stay. There was a lazy river running throughout this portion of the property. It looked so refreshing. We passed several large buildings that I presumed to be conference spaces. Each of the residences we drove by had different architecture. There were Spanish-style casitas, as well as log cabins, and also thatch-roofed small cottages scattered about. I couldn't wait to explore; my brain was having a difficult time taking everything in all at once.

"Okay, my friends. Here we are!" We pulled up to a much larger residence than I had pictured in my head. The dirt path that led to the front door was lined with rock and large planters with beautiful plants in them. There were large cottonwood trees all around providing lots of shade. Ours was one of the log cabin style—very cute. There was a covered front deck with lovely patio furniture, more planters, and a gas fire pit. As we took the few steps onto the deck, I heard water. Yes, there was also a small fountain in the corner. I think I was seeing the pattern here—all areas included the four natural elements.

Badri was quick in unloading all our bags and the water bottles into our cabin before we even made it inside. I took Shadow around the corner of the house to let her do her business since we'd had a long drive. From the backside of the house, I could see casitas and cottages off in the distance, but none of them were too close. I admired the wonderful privacy we had.

Shadow and I walked through the front door, and my eyes once again took in all the features: beautiful bamboo wood flooring, tall ceilings and windows, along with soft earth-tone colored furniture and decorations featured throughout. They didn't miss a single thing when designing this place. The spacious living area and kitchen were the first rooms inside the front door, then there were bedrooms to either side of that great room, so we each had a 'wing' as our own private space. Shadow sniffed all around and came back wagging her tail wildly; she obviously approved.

Before Badri left, he handed us each our own L&M monogrammed stainless-steel portable water bottles filled with spring water. "Drink ... drink!" he exclaimed, "Today is 'water' day and we must all stay hydrated." We both lifted the bottles to our mouth and swallowed the most delicious water I'd ever experienced. It was almost sweet in a way. I kept drinking until the container was empty, then I refilled.

"Guess I *was* thirsty..." Bella mentioned as she polished off hers too. "Living in Mesa, you don't get water this good." Badri seemed pleased. He turned to fill the bowl that I had set out on the kitchen floor for Shadow; she immediately began drinking and finished hers too.

"Anything else you need?"

"Do we get a key?"

He looked confused.

"A key to lock up while we're away from here." I motioned turning a key at the door handle.

"No, no keys. Everything is open; there's no need in a place such as this, ma'am. Ok, then. One more thing ... that button there—" he pointed to one next to the light switches inside the front door. "Press it if you need me. I'm here to serve," he bowed. When he stood straight again, he held up his index finger and said, "You have *one hour* before I come back for the tour. See you then," he bowed, backing out of the front door, and closing it.

We both stared at each other. "I'm not sure about not being able to lock up when we're away. But, wow! What a place, huh?" I looked at the front door closer and realized it wasn't just that they didn't pass out keys to guests, there was *no locking mechanism* at all. "We can't even lock the place when we're inside."

Bella didn't seem fazed at all. She breezed by, headed to the bedrooms for a look. "Fantastic! Looks like they are identical ... which one do you want?"

"I'll take the east wing?" I mimicked the super wealthy, and she laughed in agreement.

We both spent the hour getting unpacked and settling into what would be our home for the next five days. Already, I felt myself relaxing.

CHAPTER NINE

A silent retreat?" I scolded Bella, as I remembered what the check-in lady had described. We stood in our yoga wear, waiting for our shuttle. Shadow was left inside the house with a cookie and her fluffy dog bed. I could see her peeking out the window though, wondering why she couldn't go along. I prayed she didn't damage anything. I could only imagine what this place cost.

"I know, I'm sorry! I actually completely forgot about that element of the retreat." She honestly looked regretful so I eased up on her.

"How do I *not* talk for several days?" I wondered out loud, as Badri pulled up.

"Ah, yoga time!" he said in his joyful way. "You will

love it. How did you enjoy your tour and lunch with Uma earlier?"

We both recalled elements of each earlier event that we had enjoyed, then before we knew it, he had pulled up to the yoga center and said goodbye.

A gorgeous man with short, but wavy brown slicked-back hair approached us. He was also wearing loose-fitting black yoga pants and a lean gray tank top that showed off his well-toned body. "Bella!" he yelled out.

She whipped around to see who had called her name. "Hello, Joseph." She kept her tone neutral; it didn't appear to me that she particularly cared for this man. Then it dawned on me, *Ah, this was the guy—Joseph*. I stared the man up and down, having heard about him, but never having seen him before.

"Have you seen Jill, yet?" He glanced over at me. "Did she travel with you, or on her own?"

Bella shook her head and pointed to me. "This is my friend, Libby … we came together."

He nodded my direction, but continued rambling on, "I know she paid to come to this retreat, but she hasn't been answering my calls for the past week or so." He hung his head in defeat. Then, in a low voice, lifting his eyes to my friend, "Have you heard from her?"

"I haven't." She was succinct and didn't elaborate on the fact that she had found her friend's apartment empty, the day after she was last known to have been on a date with him.

Joseph abruptly turned on his full snake-oil salesman's-like charm and turned in my direction. "Well, Libby … how long have you been a member here?"

"I'm not. I'm her guest." Then I turned to Bella, "We

need to get inside, don't we? Class is about to start."

"Oh, I'm headed that way too. Please … let me be your escort," Joseph hooked both elbows as though he wanted us to link our arms through. We declined and walked off ahead of him. "Rude…" he commented under his breath, but we heard it. We kept walking.

Goosebumps had started to prickle my arms and traveled up through my scalp. I nearly bowed out of yoga to get away from this guy; there was just something about him. Was it because of the story Bella told me about his party? I wasn't sure, but I assumed I'd probably be better off inside with this group, than heading back to our little cabin alone. As soon as we had walked in, I saw Uma at the front of the class. There were only about ten people in the room when we joined. All of us wore face masks. I looked around for a tall blonde California girl, but no one matched that description.

Mr. Tech Guy set up his mat right in front, nearest to Uma. We hung out in the back of the class. Before they got started, he had pulled Uma over to the side and they were whispering with their backs to us. Only when they turned around did I feel eyes boring into me. He was pointing in our direction. I turned slightly to look over my shoulder; nope, no one there. The slime bag was pointing us out to Uma and I wanted to know why. I nudged Bella.

"Did you see that?" I whispered.

"Yeah, wonder what he told her?"

Uma began the initial breathing exercises and sun salutations to begin the class. I swore Joseph never took his eyes off me the entire time. The goosebumps never went away.

* * *

When we returned to our cabin, there was a note on the door. Uma had invited Bella and I to sit at the guru table during dinner. *Great. Just great.*

"I suppose it's the last supper where we'll be able to talk. This will be fun to visit with Uma and Kali!" Bella smiled; she was clearly excited by the invitation.

I filled my water bottle with the refreshing spring water. I noticed Shadow's bowl was empty again so I refilled hers as well. Then, I took her out for a walk before we had to shower and dress for dinner and Satsang. As we journeyed around the grounds, I found myself trying to remember what the lady earlier told us about Satsang. *What exactly are we doing tonight?* If I was correct, it was only an educational gathering. I'd have to look that up when we got back.

That thought reminded me that I hadn't removed my phone from Shadow's pouch. We stopped and I kneeled down to remove it. I turned it on and made sure that my sounds were muted. Since we were in a scenic part of the grounds, I started snapping pictures; I couldn't wait to share with Greg. I turned behind me and snapped another view. That's when I saw him—Joseph. *Oh shit! Busted with the phone.* I quickly stashed it in my back pocket. He was still some distance away from us and didn't appear to make a move to come closer so I knelt down next to Shadow pretending to focus on her paw. I could still see him and now realized it was his cottage he stood next to—he went inside. *Maybe he never saw us—or more importantly, the phone I held.* We began to walk in that direction.

As we passed by Joseph's residence, I could hear both a male and a female voice. That got me wondering, *did he bring a guest too?* Seemed odd since he was asking earlier about Jill. I thought they were an item. Or, maybe Jill *was* the voice I heard. Maybe she's here. I slowed to see if I could hear what they were saying. The voices were elevated—sounded like a disagreement, but I couldn't hear specifics. Footfalls could be heard, sounded as though one of them was pacing back and forth. Then the front door, which was opposite from where Shadow and I stood, opened and slammed a second later. We picked up our pace, nearly to a run, and turned down the next trail, which led us to the outdoor adventure area.

We didn't go all the way down the trail to where groups do those insane 'trust' activities. I was sure Shadow wouldn't be allowed there. During the tour, they demonstrated some of the leadership excursions. It's all about getting teams, or couples, learning to trust one another by completing what looked to me like death defying stunts. *No thank you!* Instead, we found that there was another trail which would lead us back near the main building; from there, we could get back to our home without running into Joseph.

Or, at least I thought so.

CHAPTER TEN

My skin crawled as soon as I heard his voice. I whipped around. He moved in way too close for my comfort level. Shadow let out a low growl which moved the creepy tech-mogul back a step or two.

"Hey, Libs," he played cool, but must have seen disgust etched on my face. "Sorry, that's your name, isn't it?"

"Libby," I corrected.

"Didn't know they allowed pets here," he commented, looking at Shadow. "What's your pup's name?" He abruptly moved to pet Shadow, but she was having none of it. She barked and scooted closer to me. "Whoa! Does she bite?"

"No, she does not. But both of us believe in personal space, so please give us some. Generally, when you approach a dog … you do it slowly, and with a sweet voice, *asking for permission.*"

"Okay, okay. Don't have to get crabby. Just trying to be friendly…" He turned and headed back the direction he came from. Then, turned and called over his shoulder, "Don't let them catch you with that cell phone!"

My heart was thumping. Sweat had formed on my brow and the palms of my hands. I knelt down to Shadow. "Thank you, girl. You're a good judge of character. We don't like that guy, do we?" I talked to her in the syrupy sweet voice she loves. As I loved on her, I removed my phone cautiously from my pocket and quickly hid it back in the secret pouch on her harness. *What are they going to do—frisk us?* It all seemed so ridiculous, but then I thought back to the humongous muscled security guard who had looked all intimidating. *I wonder what they would they do if they found 'illegal' contraband? I'm not sure I want to find out … but here we are.*

We hurried back to our cabin and I showered and got dressed for our evening out. First, dinner at the guru table—should be dandy. Then, whatever Satsang was. After my nice long hot shower, and for the first time since leaving home early this morning, I felt remarkably at peace. I couldn't explain it, but I could feel myself smiling, even when no one was around. Any tension I felt earlier from that creepy guy had melted away. I felt amazing and I was ready for this.

* * *

By the time dinner was served, I was famished. It was then I realized the few fresh-pressed juices, water, and the vegetable and grain dish we had for lunch had long since worn off.

I watched as several nice-looking waiters in tuxedos surrounded our table holding plates covered in those fancy silver domes. The one I presumed to be the head waiter, nodded to his comrades and then each of them simultaneously removed the silver hood and, all in unison, set plates in front of the eight of us at the table. I'd never seen such precision.

Once they walked away, Kali picked up her glass of wine, which I supposed was the sign that we all should follow. The rest of us lifted ours; she toasted then said, "Bon Appetit!"

The grilled salmon, vegetables, and Israeli couscous was drizzled in a creamy dill dressing and my stomach rumbled as I took in the aroma. I happened to glance around the room and realized that the tuxedoed crew had only served our table. As soon as their procession made it out of the room, numerous waitresses scurried all about to deliver food to the other ten or so tables. Guess the guru table received special choreographed food delivery. Fancy.

Even though the silence rule hadn't been implemented yet, the room was remarkably quiet, except for the tinkling sounds of the china and cutlery connecting while people ate. As soon as the meal was complete, the noise level resumed to what it was previously, with each table's guests quietly talking amongst themselves and then the occasional burst of laughter.

Kali caught me off guard as I was looking around the room. "Libby, how are you enjoying your accommodations?" she asked sweetly, but I still startled.

"Oh! It's nice here. I love it. And, thank you again for letting me bring my dog. That was extremely generous. I don't see others with their pets…"

She disregarded the part about Shadow and continued, "I hope you'll enjoy yourself and take full benefit of our retreat. You are meant to relax and embrace your inner peace. Please let us know if there's *anything* we can do to make your stay more pleasant."

I nodded and noticed that everyone at the table was staring directly at me. Aside from Uma and Kali, Bella and myself, the nice people from our shuttle were sitting with us—the older gentleman, Danny, and Katerina. Next to them were a couple who were in their seventies and appeared to me as though this wasn't their first rodeo. They seemed to fit right in and were comfortable with the whole 'guru table' bit. I smiled to all of them and addressed Uma and Kali politely.

"Yes, absolutely. I'll let you know. But, I can't imagine what else I could possibly need. You seem to have thought of everything so far!" I picked up my glass and took a sip of the delicious Pinot Noir, hoping the tuxedos would appear with more. "Oh, you know, I do have a question."

Uma chuckled, "Okay, great. What's your question, Libby?"

"What is Satsang?"

Everyone else at the table looked around at each other knowingly and gave a little snicker. I felt like, if this were yesterday, I'd have been self-conscious about their reaction, but nope, not tonight. I was much more relaxed. Uma in her soothing voice said, "Satsang is simply a gathering. Think of it as fellowship. Each night we'll gather and educate on various spiritual topics—we've got a theme for each night. Some of the evenings, we may also include song … and there may be question and answer sessions related to the lessons. Every night, we'll include meditation, of course."

Of course. "Oh, okay. So, similar to the other night when I came to the center…"

"Exactly," she smiled and her eyes softened.

Kali bowed slightly as she scooted her chair back. She gracefully stood and looked around the room. "Excuse me, my lovelies. Time to make my rounds." And, she elegantly strode to the next table and greeted each person.

I couldn't help myself; she was lovely to watch so I turned my whole body, my gaze following her moves. That's when I noticed that Joseph was sitting at the next table behind me. He, too, was captivated by her presence; staring in awe as she stood over him. Then, he looked to our table, directing his creepy little smirk at me. I swiftly turned back to my companions.

I felt a tap on my shoulder and cringed, expecting to see him standing there. To my surprise, it was Brian. I stood and gave him a warm welcome hug—so thankful it was him instead. Both of us asked each other in unison, "What are you doing here?" and then we started laughing. Bella reached out and tapped him on his side.

He turned to her smiling, "Good evening, Bella … so good to see you again. Ah, the Thompsons—you made it!" he said to the older couple at the table. Then he inched around to my left. "I'm not sure we've met. I'm Brian Gant," he reached out to shake hands with Danny, who stood and introduced himself and the young lady sitting next to him, whom he'd become familiar with. "Very nice to meet you both." Brian turned back to me. "I'm shocked seeing you here—had no idea you were into all this." His arm swept out toward the room.

"Well, you can thank Kali and Bella…" I gave a slight

eye roll. "No, really, it's lovely here—what a great place." I saw one of the tuxedos coming our way. I swiftly grabbed my empty wine glass and held it out.

"You're joining the group later … well, actually *now*, aren't you?" He looked at his watch. I looked around and noticed that many in the dining hall were now making their way toward the exits. Uma and the Thompsons had left and it looked like Danny and Katie were making a move now as well. Dangit, I couldn't take my wine with me so, in several large gulps, I downed it. So unladylike.

"Yep. Why don't Bella and I head over with you?" My head had already started to feel a bit fuzzy. It occurred to me that maybe he was here with someone so my eyes swept the room, looking for someone waiting; there was no one. By then, he had agreed he'd join us so we headed out as a trio.

"You know that after Satsang, and for the remainder of the time here, we can't talk. We all have to observe silence." He knew me too well. *How am I supposed to not talk for multiple days?*

"Yes, yes … I've been versed. Not sure how I'll do it, but okay, I'll play along." We all laughed; I felt so giddy. I knew Bella and Brian must already have bets on how long it would take to break my silence.

We followed the other guests until Bella stopped suddenly.

"Hey, it's Jill … I'll meet you in there." She ran ahead.

I never saw the girl she ran after. Brian and I lifted our masks in place as we walked into the chapel and found seats about mid-room. I looked around for Bella … Jill … or Mr. Slick, but hadn't located any of them when a chime sounded. A hush fell over the room and within seconds, the doors closed and the lights dimmed. Candles glowed all around the room. It was gorgeous and matched the warmth I felt internally. Bella slipped in beside me. I turned to her, and out of nowhere, I started giggling. At first, she looked confused, but my giddiness was contagious apparently. We couldn't look at each other without cracking up. Brian then started in, and we were done. It was that quiet 'church' effect and we were the naughty children.

From either side of the stage, both Uma and Kali appeared to float into the room. Dressed in loose-fitting, all-white linen, they looked like angels as they bowed to one another and then to their audience. I couldn't hold it in; my laugh now came out as a loud snort. Bella then snickered harder and Brian tried his best to contain himself, to quiet us, but it was impossible for me to get beyond the image of angels descending into the room. Thankfully, it appeared as though no one else had noticed our little ruckus. A gong sounded—three times. I sat up straight.

"Good evening," Kali's warm soft voice greeted. "We are so blessed to have you all here this evening. Let's get started. Our theme this retreat will be focused on nature and the earth's elements … air, water, fire, and earth. Her voice had a hypnotic effect and I no longer had the giggles. I also connected Badri's comment earlier about today's focus on being about water.

Two soft blue oversized chairs were front and center on the stage and Uma and Kali each folded themselves into a lotus position before speaking into their wireless headsets. Their voices seemed to hover above us—again, like angels speaking from heaven. Now the imagery was as comforting to me as it once was funny. I settled in listening to their message; then several breathing exercises, taking a deep dive into the meditation, and then we followed along in song before the evening session wrapped up.

Uma reminded everyone before we left the chapel that for the rest of the retreat, they respectfully asked that all patrons observe the rules of silence. We each received small pads of paper and when necessary, we could write a message. Otherwise, she assured us that through all our senses, communication was possible. We didn't need our voices to live amongst one another. *Sure, whatever.*

For our evening water activity, we were to each change into our swim wear and meet back at the spa building. When we did, we learned that we'd be enjoying the river for a nighttime float. Bella and I walked up to the platform where, after waiting for our turn, two gentlemen helped us each onto large inner-tubes in the water. I'd wondered how comfortable the water would be at night, but it was heated and felt amazing. Our arms draped along the sides of the black rings and we floated gracefully along. Resting my head back, I saw that the stars were brilliant in the night sky, and occasionally a glowing lotus flower would float by in the water.

Before we made it to the end of the river, Brian floated up and whispered, "Found you guys!" I laughed and the three of us continued tonight's relaxing exercise of 'letting go' with nature's water element. I felt no tension any longer and for the first time since agreeing to attend, I was actually grateful that I had. This was just what I needed. Perhaps once we got home, Greg and I would talk; I probably had nothing to worry about.

Our river float excursion was complete about an hour later. Everyone had assembled back at the spa building, each changing out of their wet clothes inside the locker rooms, then indulging in a warm cup of cocoa before silently walking out into the fresh night's air again.

Individuals and couples broke away from the main group as they branched off onto pathways leading back to their residences. Bella, Brian, and I walked quietly toward our cabin, sipping the delicious chocolate drink. I started to ask him where his place was, but he held his finger to his mouth, shushing me. He pointed ahead, to a cabin which was about fifty yards away from ours. As he moved away from us, he put his palms together and bowed. We did the same. *Goodnight.*

I wanted to ask Bella whether she had caught up to Jill, but I'd wait until we got inside where writing on the notepad would be easier. We had our cabin in sight and decided the evening was so nice, we'd sit in the chairs out on our deck while finishing our cocoa. I let Shadow out and she sniffed around outside the cabin and then lay at our feet. Bella lit the gas porch heater, after being a bit chilled from the water adventure earlier.

I picked up my notepad, asking my question about Jill. Bella shook her head no. My shoulders slumped. We thought for sure she'd show up here and the mystery of her disappearance would be answered.

Then, out of the silence, a shrill scream ignited the dark, still night.

CHAPTER ELEVEN

We jumped, startled. Shadow barked. "What was that..." I started to say, but Bella was already shushing me.

"C'mon, it's an emergency. I think we can make an exception." Bella seemed to contemplate that for a fraction of a second.

"Hurry!" she said, and we took off running.

A female voice continued to scream and as we got closer, I realized that this was the earlier path I'd taken, passing by Joseph's place. We rounded the corner; the screaming had ceased, and we saw there was a crowd already gathered outside one of the residences. Several men with reflective vests that read EMT pushed past us to get to someone on the ground. We couldn't get any closer, the behemoth guard and a couple of his cronies were pushing back the guests and securing a perimeter.

I looked around for familiar faces. I saw young Katie crying and wondered if she was the screamer we heard. She seemed distraught; it's possible that she saw something. Danny was whispering with another gentleman I didn't recognize not far away. No sign of Joseph, or the gurus. Everyone in the group was whispering amongst one another. Like I told Bella, apparently there *were* exceptions for breaking the rules.

One of the EMTs used his shoulder radio to instruct someone at the other end. We couldn't hear specifics from where we were, but overall, it didn't look good. The mood amongst the first responders appeared solemn. Shadow was getting antsy, shifting back and forth on her feet, so she and I ventured away from the crowd. She sniffed around and pulled me into some trees not far away. We could no longer see the crowd, but I could hear voices through the shrubbery and not far away from us. A woman. I strained to hear what she was saying and whether I recognized the voice.

"I told you to get rid of her!"

"I thought I *had*…" The man's voice was familiar, but whose? "Don't worry, I've covered our tracks well."

The woman hissed, *"Ours?"*

Footfalls sounded, crunching leaves, and they were moving off into the distance. Shadow and I followed; I wanted to see. We picked up speed when I could no longer hear steps or their voices. When we came to the next intersection, I looked left—no one could be seen. I snapped my head right—no one there either. The path didn't continue forward so I chose to go right. We walked until the lighted walk circled back around and we found ourselves right back at the scene of the incident.

Bella looked concerned. "Where did you go?"

"Shadow had to go … and, then, I got turned around. Have you learned anymore?"

She shook her head. Our attention was diverted when they started moving the ever-growing crowd again. The EMTs had a body on a gurney and were trying to get down the path. As they passed by us, we saw a still body under a white sheet. Bella gasped.

"What?" I asked her quietly as the gurney passed within a foot of us.

She began to cry, and she pointed. I saw a slender wrist dangling off the side—there was a tattoo. "It's her…" she gasped for breath. I pulled her away and we walked in silence back to our cabin.

* * *

The previous night had been a long one as I tried to console Bella. She was sure it was Jill on that gurney and we both figured the outcome was not a good one. Although we hadn't heard one way or another, we wondered why the body had been fully covered. I kept reminding Bella that we don't know anything for certain, so we need to remain positive.

Badri came calling around seven o'clock when it was time for sunrise yoga. Although neither of us were all that enthused, we had decided not to sit around the cabin any longer either. We had already dressed in our finest yoga wear, grabbed our mats, and climbed aboard Badri's cart when it arrived.

"Good morning, my guests … did you sleep well?" he

cheerfully asked.

We looked at each other wondering if it was a trap. I wrote out on my notepad. *Good morning ... why are you not in silence, too?* I ripped off the small paper and reached over his shoulder to hand it to him. He pulled the cart aside then quickly read the note. He turned around to us and bowed Namaste, giving us a look of apology for disturbing our silence. Then we took off down the path again.

Both Bella and I lowered our heads as we passed the somber area where someone was injured, or possibly even died, last night. I could see her eyes well up again; I put my arm around her for comfort. Badri pulled up to the beautiful grassy area where outside yoga was being held this morning. He got out to help us off the cart, then smiled and bowed again before taking off. We each found a space among the other guests and laid out the mats, taking our seats. The gong sounded.

My mind raced through most of the session. *What had happened last night? Was there a killer on the loose?* I had to push visions of Joseph from my head. Or, perhaps someone had a medical emergency—we didn't know for sure. *Was it Jill?* I sure hoped they'd give us some kind of update. But, all of it—Bella's concern before coming here to presumably seeing her friend removed on a stretcher—it reeked of suspicion. I needed JJ's help—my detective friend might be able to learn more. Certainly, the body they removed the night before would be sent to the Medical Examiner for an autopsy. If that was in Phoenix, JJ could ask questions. If it was Tucson, I wasn't so sure. After ruminating, I was pleasantly surprised that our hour yoga session was already over. Another gong sounded as we laid in Savasana—my favorite part of yoga—sprawled on my back in relaxation.

Several minutes went by before others began to move. Reluctantly, I did too. We gathered our mats, wiped sweat from our faces, and steadied ourselves for the next activity.

We didn't call for Badri and opted for a nice meditative walk instead, over to the cute chapel for morning meditation. We walked in silence; I had to giggle at the scene—the group looked like sheep blindly following. I finished drinking the cool water from my water container, all the while playfully thinking, *hopefully, we weren't being led to our slaughter.* I giggled.

Inside, we ingested the sweet green shot when we arrived. Incense was burning, sunlight cast a spectrum of colors throughout the room from the stained-glass windows. It sure didn't feel like a slaughter—I felt warm and comforted in this room. All my anxiety and doubt had melted away. Another gong sounded and everyone found a seat. Silence was all around; the only sounds were the shuffling of feet. I closed my eyes as the remaining tones from the gong lingered in the air.

When I opened my eyes again, Kali and Uma were already perched in their cozy seats on the stage. They softly gazed around the room, and once the back doors quietly closed, Kali's hushed voice sounded.

"Welcome everyone. Before we begin, we feel it's important to be transparent with all members. There was an emergency last night, as some of you well know. Before the rumor mill gets too far down the rails, we want to address the facts." She bowed her head slightly before allowing Uma to continue.

Bella shifted in her seat and I felt her tension.

Uma cleared her throat. "My lovelies. Last night one of our members had a medical emergency. For the sake of privacy, we will not give details—including which member. However, we can say that the individual was airlifted from here and is receiving the best medical care possible as we speak. In time, only with the permission of the person, or their family, we may share more. We know you all will want to hold space for her, or him, in your prayers so be assured, we'll let you know as soon as we are able. Until then, this morning's meditation is dedicated to love and light—please, let's all focus our loving and positive energy to healing. To healing our member, our hearts, our souls. Please close your eyes..."

I looked to Bella to see if she was comforted by the guru's message; her eyes were already closed. I gently closed mine too. At first my mind seemed to be racing—thinking through the possibilities of what could have happened to the poor soul. I was sure it was a woman; the slight wrist we saw—didn't appear to be a man, to me. It didn't take long before Kali's soothing voice forced all other thoughts away. I drifted, seeing colorful lights swirling; visions that came and went, and only disappeared when the soft chime sounded from some distant place. Thirty minutes had passed like seconds. Eventually, I slowly opened my eyes and took in the surroundings. Everything was peaceful.

As Bella stood, my body felt as though it was on autopilot; blindly following my friend—mimicking her moves. She scrawled on her pad and handed it to me. *Let's stop for juice ... then head back for showers?* I nodded and we walked into the main building where we found other members who had the same idea. It was completely silent as we waited; the only sound was the constant whir of the juicer mutilating fruits and vegetables.

I found myself entranced by the juice making process,

but slowly my attention diverted to the bright colors and flowing material several yards away—the gurus glided on through the main front doors. The energy in the room elevated, even though no one spoke a word. Several members passed by, bowing to the gurus, and they returned the favor. By the time they had walked the entire length of the building and out the glass doors at the other end, it was our turn to place our orders. Bella went first, handing over a sheet of paper where she had written down her order. My gaze drifted outside.

Brian had stopped the gurus and it appeared to me they were talking. No notepads that I could see. *Why were they talking? Look, they're breaking their own rules.* I didn't feel so guilty then. My attention was caught by something else. Brian looked visibly upset. I'd never seen him bothered so it was quite apparent, and I wondered whether it was what they said, or …

Bella tapped my shoulder to get my attention. I whipped around and saw it was my turn, so I smiled and handed the girl my piece of paper. I turned back around and the three I'd been watching outside were no longer there. *I wonder what that was all about.* I grabbed my juice and we set off to our place.

* * *

Once we were safely inside our place, Bella wrote another note and handed it to me. I immediately broke the silence.

"What! We are doing *what* next?"

Shhhhh, she mimicked.

"No! We're in our own cabin … and I'm going to talk.

You mean to tell me that we all have to climb that pole and participate in *group trust?*"

She frowned. "Ok. No one will force you, but I thought you always loved adventure and trying new stuff?"

"Did you *see* what they demonstrated yesterday? It looks horrifying." On the other hand, I supposed she did have a point. After all, I've gone sky diving … certainly, I could do this.

We showered and then I took Shadow for a long walk. The activity session was later in the afternoon and I wasn't going to waste my peaceful glow yet. Ever since last evening's meditation session, I'd found myself feeling so calm. Except for the excitement of hearing someone screaming and seeing a stretcher hauling someone away, I've felt remarkably peaceful here. Maybe I *could* see myself doing this more—I think I understood Bella and Lexi and their love of the place a little better now.

Katie was walking toward us. I really wanted to talk to her; what did she see last night? I forgot my notepad, but I stopped and bowed hello. When she stopped too, I sensed she might want to talk. We both looked around us cautiously. I stepped closer.

"I saw you at the scene last night. Are you okay?" I whispered.

Tears sprung immediately. I gave her a hug and Shadow sat on her feet, rubbing up against her. She petted the pup. Finally, she mouthed, "I'll be fine…"

"Can you tell me what you saw?"

Paranoid, she looked all around us again, ensuring no one was witnessing our conversation. She took my hand and led Shadow and me down the path. We walked up to another super cute dwelling which looked like a little thatched cottage. She opened the door and we went inside.

"Libby, how long has Bella been a member?" she asked me, still looking at the window as though someone may have followed us.

"Um. Well, I believe only a few months. At most."

She invited me to sit in the small living room.

"And you are her guest, right?"

I nodded.

"You have *not* started paying dues or anything … you are in the honeymoon phase, right?"

I nodded again, slowly; starting to get concerned over her questioning.

"I've been a member for years. It's changed a *lot* in the past year."

"How? What do you mean?"

"It's difficult to say exactly how. But, I can tell you that it's not the Love & Mercy I joined years back."

"Can you give me an example?" I could tell she was giving me the once-over, assessing how much she should divulge.

"For one, they appear to be dividing families— separating parents from children. Power over members— maybe blackmail even. Money seems to be *the* driving factor. Maybe it was all along, I don't know."

"Are you talking about the course costs?"

She hung her head. Her shoulders started to heave before her voice cracked, "*Everything.* Courses, retreats, membership dues … you name it. Many members now work for the organization to pay off their debt. I am in debt for thousands…" her watery eyes looked up to mine, "*tens of thousands* of dollars. I have no idea what I'm going to do."

I put an arm around her. I didn't quite know what to say—was there anything that could make her situation better?

After spilling more tears, she looked embarrassed. "I know what you're thinking— stop, leave the group." Her head turned to me, her face was beet red. "*I can't*. The girl—well, woman—she was in her twenties, the one last night," Katie became fidgety, stood up, and began to pace around. "I'm afraid she wanted out—she couldn't pay her debts."

"Who was the girl? Was it Jill?"

She stopped in her tracks and confusedly looked over to me. "Who? No. Her name is Bonnie. Who's Jill?"

Silently thankful that it wasn't Bella's friend, I dismissed the Jill subject and tried comforting Katie to keep her talking. "Bella's friend. Did you see what happened to Bonnie?"

She started bawling. Finally, she nodded. "I think she was poisoned. We'd gone for a walk and she wasn't feeling good ... you know, after Satsang last night. We both thought it was her system getting used to the fiber-rich diet they serve." She looked up again, "I don't do as well with this diet at home—love things like tacos and pizza too much," she smiled innocently. "Anyway, we were making our way back here so she could use my restroom, it was the closest. But, she didn't make it. She fell to the ground and started writhing, holding her stomach, and white foam-like..." she caught her breath, "started coming out the sides of her mouth. I wasn't sure if she was having a seizure or what. I completely panicked. All I could do was scream ..."

I stood up and pulled her into my arms. "It's not your fault, Katie. And, maybe she did have a seizure—some ailment no one knew about? It's hard to know what to do in these situations. Don't worry, sweetie, as Kali said earlier, she'll be fine."

Shadow barked. There was a knock at the door. Katie jumped and her eyes flew open wide. Nervously, she peeked out the window. With her finger up to her mouth warning me to be quiet, "Oh shit! It's that Joseph guy…" she mouthed.

My heart leapt. *What's he doing here?*

"I heard you in there, Katie!" he yelled. "Not like you and Libby can hide with a barking dog."

She carefully opened the door and he pushed through, closing the door, and giving me the side-eye as he did. Shadow growled, but I pulled her close.

"What are you girls up to in here? Not being silent, that's for sure." His ominous laugh made my skin crawl.

"Doesn't sound like you are being silent either—yelling outside there," I pointed to the door.

He didn't appear to appreciate me pointing out the obvious. We stared each other down for an uncomfortable moment, then he turned to Katie.

"I was coming by to make sure you're okay," he held out his hand to Katie; she declined it. "Hey, I know you were upset last night. Your friend will be okay. We're here for you."

She walked to the door, holding it open. "Thank you for coming by, Joseph. I'm fine. Libby is here."

He got the hint and turned toward the door. "No more talking, ladies." Shadow lunged and barked at him. He jumped across the threshold and glared at me. "That dog shouldn't be here. He's dangerous!"

I didn't say anything, what was the use of correcting

him anyway. Once we observed him walk down the path, assured he was long gone, we both shivered as though we were shaking him off. Shadow still appeared to be on guard, not budging from the window.

"Who is that guy, anyway?" I asked. "I mean, I know he was Jill's boyfriend, but … who does he think he is—all creepy and gross. He acts as though he runs the place or something."

"I know. What was that? As though he's here on behalf of the gurus? Sheesh!" Katie huffed. "I heard he started with us because his company forced him into leadership training—or anger management, or something like that. But all I've seen him do is cozy up to the gurus and yes, on occasion, he acts as though he's running the place." She tsked and shook her head in disgust. "Wait. You said 'his girlfriend' … oh, *that Jill?* I didn't know her by name, but I think I know who you are talking about now. Tall, blonde … beautiful, from California?"

"Yes! Have you seen her?" I got excited, hoping to take back some positive news to Bella.

She thought for a second. "I swore I saw her yesterday. But, then, I can't be sure. You know, ever since I've arrived here, things seem a tad foggy. I know I've long since needed a retreat, but I never imagined how much so until we arrived."

She thanked me for taking the time to console her and we both agreed it was time to go back into silence. As Shadow and I walked back to the cabin, I considered everything Katie had divulged. She was up to her eyeballs in debt to this organization. She's fearful of Joseph. The member injured last night was Bonnie, not Jill. And, what was the mention about separating kids and parents? I'd have to follow up more on that later—seemed unlikely that parents would agree to be separated. Not sure how that would work. From everything I'd observed so far, it seemed unlikely that the organization was responsible for anything other than maybe price gouging.

But, isn't that the fault of those signing up and agreeing to pay such exorbitant fees? Seems to me that you say 'no' and find a better place for self-help. Psychologists could be a cheaper option, perhaps. Or, pick up one of the many millions of books out there covering every self-help subject imaginable. Didn't sound difficult to me.

CHAPTER TWELVE

I cannot believe you talked me into doing this." The afternoon was warm, but a light layering of clouds prevented it from being hot. I heard Shadow bark from below. I hesitantly glanced the fifty feet down to earth and quickly looked forward again. Bella was fixed, unmoving, to the tiny platform. We each separately had climbed an impossibly tall, swaying wooden pole to get where we were.

"This is terrifying…" she muttered, not moving a muscle.

The bullhorn sounded from below. We were instructed to turn and face one another, to tell one another what we value about the other, and then holding hands we were to jump off the platform together. Neither of us budged. After a few minutes, the bullhorn squawked again demanding that we get started, others were waiting their turn.

With the tiniest baby steps, we shuffled our feet on the platform to point toward each other. The pole began a gradual sway; our eyes reflected the terror we felt as we turned to face each other; we reached out and held hands.

Gripping tight, I whispered to Bella, "I value your bravery."

She grimaced a smile and said back, "I value your humor and …" Before she could finish, she had caught a glimpse of the ground. She startled and suddenly all I heard was, "friennndshippp…" as we hurtled towards earth. I squeezed my eyes together tight.

I ricocheted upwards nearly as high as we'd been on the platform, when the bungy cord recoiled; my harness was impossibly tight and binding my pelvic area. She screamed loudly as my friend whizzed by opposite of me, coming close to colliding as we swung past each other again. We continued to bounce around in the air for a few moments, fortunately not slamming into anything, when I realized that we were laughing wildly. Soon, our guides assisted us from our harnesses as our jellied legs tried to remain standing. Brian was nearby holding Shadow on her leash. As soon as I was sure my legs would hold me, I walked over to them. I bowed with prayer hands to him as a thank you and he handed me Shadow's leash.

I knelt down to my baby, scratching behind her ears and finally sitting on the ground with her. I whispered quietly in her ears, so thankful that I was back on earth with my girl. That was utterly terrifying, but equally exhilarating. I couldn't wait to talk about it with Bella once we were behind our four walls—for now, we were supposed to remain silent. Our assignment for today was to pay attention to all our senses as we explore the earth's air element. I looked over to Bella who was also on the ground—lying down, with her eyes closed. When she opened them, she gave me a huge smile. She was okay, simply savoring the moment.

Pair by pair, all of the retreat guests took their turns in what seemed like death defying tasks. Even the gurus participated; although, I suspected all this was old hat to them. Uma and Joseph took the dive together. So did Kali and another woman I hadn't met yet, but had seen around. Katie and Danny walked dueling tightropes together. Brian and an older gentleman I'd seen around climbed the same poles we did, but had a slightly different task to complete before the jump. It was too bad these activities took place during the silent retreat because the adrenaline really hyped everyone up and all we wanted to do was *talk* about it. Even so, the staffers filled everyone's water bottles and encouraged us to hydrate well once the stunts were completed. I found myself remarkably calm and satisfied by the time everyone was done and we headed back to our place.

* * *

While Bella showered, I took the opportunity to check my phone. Luckily last night I had remembered to remove it from Shadow's harness, charge it, and find a new hiding place. There were five missed calls from Greg—I listened to the messages. *Had I not told him I'd be at this retreat?* It was a bit of a last-minute decision to join Bella; getting things settled at the spa and heading out of town, but I swore I had at least left a message for him. Listening to the playback, he sounded sad. I'd have to call him back soon. For now, I wanted to get a text message off to JJ. Could he help learn about Bonnie's hospitalization? Was there anything in the news related to this incident? I felt so isolated. After quickly sending the note, I ensured all the phone's bells and whistles were silenced and then I stuffed the phone under the mattress.

After both Bella and I had showered, I was finally able to update her on my conversation with Katie. She did not believe that Love & Mercy separated families and was super relieved to learn that it wasn't Jill injured the night before, and also that the member hadn't died, although she wasn't sure who Bonnie was. We both were curious about the woman's condition at the hospital, and what caused the episode. I told her all about Joseph showing up and we both agreed that we were leery of him, and even more so now, considering the fear Katie also displayed. *Who was this guy?*

"I meant to ask her if Danny was her father…" I started to say. Bella was already shaking her head.

"No. He's a member here—an older gentleman who had lost his way after losing his daughter. Remember, she introduced him on the van as a 'friend.' And once I overheard him saying that Katie reminds him so much of his daughter. I'm sure that's the draw. But, that's it … just friends."

"And, Katie … I was surprised to learn she wasn't from the Phoenix area, but from the Bronx, New York. I mean, yes, I hear the strong accent in her voice, but assumed that she'd been part of the Mercy Mesa chapter."

"No, I've met her recently—although I had been admiring how she's a J-Lo lookalike for a while. She's visiting at the Mesa center throughout the summer—studying. I think she has planned to return to New York after this retreat."

"I really like her. Tough, but you can see the vulnerability too. There's definitely more to her story and I'm hoping to talk to her more. It'd be easier if we didn't have to sneak around to talk. Hey, we have the rest of the afternoon free, don't we?"

Bella nodded, grabbing her journal from the counter. "I'm using it for reflective time," she smiled as she moved toward her bedroom. I was still surprisingly energized from the earlier activity, so Shadow and I left Bella to reflect.

Several people had the same idea as we did, and it was no wonder. The day was gorgeous and the silence on the grounds was calming. Per earlier instructions, I found myself focusing on the air around me and the sound it made through the trees, the feel of it on my face as I stood watching one of the many water features. Shadow seemed tranquil, watching the calming waters as well, which was different. Usually, I'd fight to keep her from jumping into a body of water. I closed my eyes, using my other senses to feel. After a few minutes, I felt Shadow move slightly. The hair on my arms tickled. When I softly opened my eyes, standing much too close to me, was Joseph.

CHAPTER THIRTEEN

Turn in that phone yet?" The air from his whisper in my ear sent alarms radiating throughout my body.

I pushed him away from me. "Personal space, *please*." My voice was stern and loud. I didn't care if we weren't supposed to talk. He was creeping me out. "What do you want from me?" I asked.

"I want you to obey the rules." He smirked and walked away.

I turned to my black Lab. "Why, why didn't you bark and scare him away? Or, at the very least, give me warning." I knelt down and hugged her. She didn't take her eyes off of him until he disappeared from her sight.

As I rose, I observed Uma leading a contingency of maybe ten women—actually, I'd say they were girls. They looked quite young. I stood and watched to see where they were headed. Shadow and I waited until they were farther away, then we followed. From what I could tell, they appeared to be in uniform—school field trip? Or, maybe they weren't *that* young—maybe they were the new staff shift today? Something made me curious though, so we casually walked along the paths much farther than we had previously, all the way to what I presumed was the gurus' residence.

It occurred to me I hadn't actually known where the gurus resided—that wasn't included in our welcome tour yesterday. This *had* to be it. The place was enormous and ornate—practically a palace. Stone stairs led up to a huge covered patio. Statues lined the front entryway, along with lush green foliage and beautiful flowers all around. The procession of girls followed the brilliant redhead into a door at the far end of the residence. We walked slightly closer, cautiously, feeling the need to remain hidden. I realized that this building was actually two separate residences. The door Uma walked into was at the south end, but there was a north end door as well. Each building was divided by a long breezeway that connected the two, as well as one long veranda facing our direction.

Shadow and I continued along the path so I could see the far south end where the group had disappeared into the building. My pup was oddly slow, without much energy. We stood on the dirt path and I could see the gathering of people inside through a large picture window. Shadow laid down at my feet. I found myself transfixed wondering what would happen if I went and knocked on the door. *Would I be invited in?* Something within me thought, *no, we wouldn't.* Then, I startled when Uma looked out the window, directly at me. I suddenly felt like a voyeur; doing something dirty and wrong. She held my gaze, then abruptly pulled the curtains across, preventing anymore ogling.

"C'mon Shadow, we've got to go." She grudgingly got up, and just in time. The ginormous security guard was on the move. Directly toward us.

We picked up speed and I resisted looking behind me all the way back to our cabin.

* * *

Bella was asleep when we walked in so Shadow and I tiptoed into our bedroom. On the way past the kitchen counter, I noticed that Badri had delivered two more five-gallon jugs of fresh water. How much were we drinking? Seemed like an awful lot.

Shadow laid down on her bed in the corner and I pulled out my phone from under the mattress before I sprawled out on my bed. I checked for messages and saw Greg had texted.

Where are U? U Okay?

My heart sank. I felt guilty—but honestly, I'd been busy and hadn't purposely tried to shut him out. I texted back:

Bella and I are at a meditation retreat. How are you? Where are you?

While I waited for a reply, I checked email. Nothing from JJ, and really, not much that I've missed within the past twenty-four hours. Good. It was nice to be away for a restful weekend. Alexis was kind to handle everything at work so we could get away.

I lay there daydreaming, periodically checking to see if Greg had answered me since my sounds were turned off. I drifted off for a while, but then remembered the pictures I was taking yesterday when I got busted by Mr. Creepo. My eyes flew open and I pulled up my pictures on the phone. There were three ... in one, it showed how beautifully lush the grounds were—grass, trees, and in the distance a wooden structure—a log cabin similar to ours. I swiped to the next photo; it was of the same structure but zoomed in on the pathway and residence. Someone was standing there—a man. Oh, and a woman, too.

I used my fingers on the phone's screen to zoom in a little more. It made it quite fuzzy, but I could tell the woman was blonde and as tall as the man. *Who was this man?* It didn't look like Joseph; I could determine that because he had a lighter hair color. He was wearing a ball cap—white and there was some type of logo on it. Perhaps the logo for Mercy? Maybe they were staffers—it was hard to say. The next photo I swiped to was clearly Joseph. He was standing on the pathway, not immediately in front of that cabin, but I could still see the edge of it. He was staring directly at me. The two from the previous picture were no longer there. I got chills.

I heard Bella starting to stir from the other side of our place. I quickly shut down the phone and replaced it under the mattress. Greg had never responded.

Shadow was completely knocked out and didn't hear me move to the living room. Bella filled her container with more water and sat down beside me.

"Nice nap?" I asked.

"Weird dreams. Did you have strange dreams last night?"

"No, I don't remember. But, I know I slept like a log."

"Hey, I saw what could have been school children earlier. Would they bring kids here for field trips or something?" I still wasn't sure they were as young as school children, but thought I'd ask.

She slowly shook her head, but gave me an inquisitive look.

"Seemed like they were following Uma into what I assume are the guru's quarters. Huge palace-like place...?"

Her brows furrowed in question. "Where's that?"

I explained the general direction I followed them to, but she knew nothing about the place or the presumed tour. She actually looked like she didn't feel well. Or, maybe was still half asleep.

"Are you okay?" I asked, reaching out to touch her forehead.

"Think I'm just tired." She took another drink from her water bottle. "That earlier activity really took it out of me, I guess."

I looked at my watch and it was nearly time. "Are you going to feel like having dinner?" I asked her.

"I'm going to go take another shower. Hopefully that will wake me up." She slowly stood. I was concerned watching her gradually make her way, slightly hunched over, the few feet into the bathroom. She really didn't look well.

I peeked back into my bedroom and Shadow hadn't budged at all. Out like a light.

* * *

On my walk to the dining hall, I ran into Brian along the path.

"Hey, where's your roomie?" he asked quietly, only after looking around for others. We appeared to be alone.

I whispered back, "Not feeling well tonight. I'm on my own."

"Aw, that's too bad. I think something is going around though, I heard Katie telling Danny earlier after the tight-rope walking that she wasn't feeling great."

"Maybe that was a little too much for all of us?" Remembering back to the queasy feeling I had while swaying on a tiny platform fifty feet off the ground, I shuddered.

"It wasn't that bad. I'm looking forward to the next one!"

I glared in his direction.

We hushed. Several more people merged from their walkways onto the path in front of us. Brian held up his notepad and I nodded in understanding, but we didn't try to write and walk at the same time.

We were all lined up waiting for the dining room doors to open when I caught sight of the gargantuan guard that filled up my periphery. If it were Christmas time, I'd swear he was gearing up to play Santa. He had a huge bundle thrown over his shoulder and he was high-tailing it behind buildings and in the general direction of the front gate, although, that would be half a mile or so away. Unable to help myself, I stepped out of the line and crept around the dining hall hoping to see where he went. Around the chapel building about twenty yards away, I skirted along the building and peeked around the other end. I jumped when I realized that Brian had followed me.

"What are you doing, Libby?" he whispered.

"Ah, geez, Brian! You lost our place in line!" His stare intensified, waiting for an answer.

"That guard," I pointed off into the distance. "He's been acting awfully suspicious. What's in that bag?"

Brian shrugged. "Taking out the laundry?"

Hmmm. Maybe.

We watched him greet a large truck. The metal rolling door lifted and the guard hefted what seemed to be a heavy load off his shoulders and onto the truck. The doors were pulled down and off it went. The guard started back in our direction.

"Libby. Dinner." Brian tugged at the sleeve of my shirt to get my attention. "Let's go!"

"Brian, how well do you know these people?"

"I've been coming here for retreats for over a year. Why?"

"Katerina—er, Katie—seems to think the organization has changed a lot over the past year. Do you feel the same?"

He shook his head. "How … how has it changed?"

I was trying to remember everything she told me. He wouldn't probably know about family separation since he was single.

"The costs—it seems she's smothered in debt because of the course fees and *mandatory* retreat? Is that true?"

"I don't know what her circumstance is, but I haven't felt pressure to take courses. I sign up because I want to and I can afford to. Hmm … mandatory retreat? That doesn't sound right."

I nodded. As much as I originally wanted to believe that Mercy could be sinister—I haven't actually *felt* that since I'd been here. In fact, I've been more at peace than ever. I looked to my friend—he seemed at peace too. No fear. But, didn't I sense that Katie had fear? Why—what was she fearful of exactly? My gaze drifted down, trying to make sense of everything, when I saw it.

I reached out and took his arm. On the inside of his wrist was an infinity symbol. "Have you had this long? I didn't remember you had tattoos." I smiled.

He laughed. "I have several. Wanna see?"

Since I could only visibly see the eternal symbol, I figured that meant the removal of clothing to show me.

"Umm, no. Only wondered." Starting to feel a little uncomfortable about the direction we were headed in the conversation, I turned back toward the dirt path. "We should get to dinner before all the food is gone," I laughed.

We walked quickly and discovered we had only missed appetizers. We took our seats at a table immediately inside the doors without much notice. I scanned the room and saw the guru table filled with tonight's honorees—those blessed enough with an invitation. Of course, Joseph was one of them. I didn't recognize any of the others.

Everyone was silently eating; a few were writing notes to one another. It appeared that the dining hall had fewer guests tonight. Of course, Bella was out. I didn't see Katie. Eventually, I saw Danny a couple tables away and he nodded as I caught his eyes. The Thompsons whom I'd met last night were nowhere to be seen. Interesting. After our scrumptious tofu, vegetables with a Tunisian-spiced quinoa, and fruit for dessert, we all filed into the chapel for meditation and Satsang again. I felt the instant warmth again after accepting the bright orange shot du jour.

I looked up, as we took our seats three rows away and was absolutely shocked to see who Kali was leading to the stage.

CHAPTER FOURTEEN

She smiled at Kali, then gracefully took her seat. Kali bowed to her to take the lead. She picked up the mallet at the side of her chair and sounded the gong. Waiting patiently as the final tones diminished and the gathering of people had settled into their seats, her melodious voice spoke, "Welcome everyone. My name is Alexis Johnson and I am honored to lead tonight's meditation. Guru Kali Patel will guide us through Satsang shortly. Now, would everyone please close your eyes. Breathing deeply…"

She guided us, but I was completely distracted by the fact that she was even here. Why hadn't she told me? I had checked the phone earlier and there was nothing from Lexi. Eventually, I settled in and allowed my friend's presence to comfort rather than surprise me. I couldn't wait to talk to her afterward.

* * *

I glanced at my watch and saw it was nearing nine o'clock. Lexi was still quietly conversing with Kali at the side of the stage. She saw me signal that I'd be by the chapel doors. I waited patiently.

I could see several cleaning staffers approaching the doors, and once they came inside, Kali and Lexi began to head my direction. I bowed to the guru, who smiled at me as she passed through the door. My friend and I watched her disappear into the night.

"What are you doing here? Loved your session, by the way," I whispered and gave her a huge hug.

"I sent you a text earlier, but I'm guessing they're keeping you plenty busy here. Yeah, they asked me last minute to fill in for Uma. Something came up, apparently."

We made our way out and headed down the path.

"They took phones from guests when we arrived," I answered.

"Then how'd you message JJ?" she asked.

I explained about how I didn't follow the rules and I got a good chuckle from her. "Sounds precisely like the good ole Libby!"

"Are you here for the remainder of the retreat?"

"Nah, just tonight."

"Certainly, you're not driving back this late, right? Where will you stay?"

"Oh, no … Kali has asked me to stay with her. I guess her place is huge. I'll get the next van back to the valley tomorrow morning." She stopped and turned to me. "Hey, don't worry… don't look so disappointed! I haven't spent much time with Kali; we'll see each other back at home. And, most importantly—you're supposed to be *silent* …

that would never work with the two of us staying together." We laughed and then quickly hushed as a couple walked past us.

"Oh, speaking earlier of the text you sent JJ …" She reached into the tote bag she was carrying, pulled out an envelope, and handed it to me. "He asked me to give this to you. Not sure what he's sent you here, but he did mention that the woman you were concerned about didn't make it. I'm so sorry. What happened?"

Sorrow engulfed me. I hadn't met the girl, but I knew how this news would be received by Katie. I couldn't believe she'd died. I told Lexi about Bonnie's incident. We both walked in silence toward the guru palace.

"Libby, are you okay? I mean, how are things going here?" She spread her arms to indicate the retreat as a whole. "And, where's Bella?"

Brain fog began to creep over me and I started to feel the exhaustion from the day's events. "I'm fine. Maybe tired. We've done so much since we arrived. I think Bella felt the same—she wasn't feeling great, so she bowed out of tonight's activities. Maybe I should have done the same?" My brow began to bead with sweat.

"Yeah, you don't look too hot, my friend. You go get some rest. I'll see you at morning yoga; I don't think the van leaves until after breakfast." We hugged and she turned away. After only a couple steps, she said, "Hey, JJ said to keep checking your messages. He's on to something else you'd be interested in … said you should hear from him tomorrow."

I smiled and nodded, but felt the distinct need to get home *now*. My pace slowed considerably as I made my way down the now familiar pathways. My stomach churned; I had nearly made it to the walkway leading to our cabin, but ended up retching in the bushes. *Where the hell had this come from?* I thought back to dinner. I had no alcohol at all—it wasn't served at tonight's meal. I had water and, of course, the cleansing shot. *It must really be working then. I suppose if this is to rid toxins, it was a good thing?*

I opened the door, ran right past Bella sprawled out on the floor, and immediately to the bathroom.

Several minutes later, I all but crawled out to the living room floor. I looked to my roommate; her coloring was as white as a sheet of paper.

She moaned, "Oh, no ... not you, too?"

The rest of the night was miserable for both of us, but eventually we fell asleep and slept right through the next morning's yoga session.

* * *

Walking into the dining hall later the next morning, I didn't see Lexi anywhere. Surprisingly, both Bella and I felt refreshed and were hungry again. Judging by last night, I was surprised we could even stand up, much less ever *want* to eat again. Maybe it meant we were clearing toxins after all? I felt great.

Brian was chipper and approached each of us with a huge embrace and invited us to sit with him at his table. He pulled out his notepad and wrote down that Lexi couldn't wait any longer, the van driver waited as long as he could. I was sad, but understood. She needed to get back to the spa while it was still early in the day. In a reply, I asked where he went after Satsang last night and how his night went. He shrugged, looking over my shoulder distracted, and never answered. I figured he might be too embarrassed to admit he was now cleansed too.

Bella excused herself to gather with a group at another table. I hadn't met any of them before, but it appeared she knew them. That's when I remembered about the news of Bonnie. I hadn't told Bella the night before. When I looked over in her direction again, I could see that she'd just received the news. Brian caught my 'ugh' and arched his brows as a question. I picked up the notepad and wrote: Bonnie died.

I was caught off guard by his reaction. His eyes sped around the room—clearly looking for someone. He got agitated and then excused himself. I watched him run straight out of the dining hall and, looking through the window, it appeared he was headed back toward his residence. All I could think was that the news upset him. I'd catch up with him later, when no one else was around, he might need someone to talk it out.

Once I'd finished my oatmeal and fruit, I made my way back to the chapel for morning meditation. This session was far busier this morning. Per the standard protocol we'd become accustomed to, all the participants were lined up getting their temperature taken as we filed in. The normal reading on the device scanned at my forehead confirmed that last night's episode wasn't anything serious. I looked around the room and found Bella was still with her tribe, and I didn't see Brian. I decided to hang out near the back today; Katie sat down next to me not long after I'd settled in. I wrote a quick: Are you okay?

She nodded and I realized she'd not heard the news yet. I'd decided to wait until later, but then Kali beat me to it. She delivered the somber news in her opening remarks and asked us to pray for Bonnie. Katie ran out in tears. I saw Uma's eyes following her.

Meditation was difficult. My mind kept veering off course—feeling sad for Katie, Bonnie's family, and everyone who knew her. So many thoughts popping up. I wondered what had affected Bella and me so strongly last night—had we eaten something bad? My eyes flew open— *where had I put that envelope Lexi gave me?*

As the session came to an end, we learned that Uma had brought in a world-renowned yogi who specialized in techniques for firing up the metabolism. Everyone around the room seemed to get excited about the news so I figured I should probably check it out later. Kali also informed us that we couldn't miss tonight's activity—she considered it the best part of the whole retreat. And with that, we filed out and went our separate directions.

I walked amongst the paths, keeping my eyes open for Brian, but ran into Danny instead. His eyes were red; it looked like he had been crying. I touched his arm and signaled 'hug' as a question. Affirming that it was okay, I embraced him, quietly asking if there was somewhere he'd like to go talk. He nodded and led the way.

Through the trees and tall brush, he led me to a large labyrinth made from stones. I had no idea this was here. It was beautiful and serene. No one was around as we quietly walked along each path. Finally, he said hushed, "I lost her five years ago—my daughter. Her name was Emily and she was the light of my life. Thirty-one was far too young." His voice caught and we walked quietly for a few minutes before he continued.

"She was over the moon about finishing her courses at Love & Mercy. Her mother and I never considered being concerned. She seemed to be thriving and I never saw it coming. They told us it was suicide. I've never believed that—not even for one second." He turned to me, his eyes burrowing into mine. "She would *never* have taken her own life."

I held back the tears that were brewing. "Is that why you're here, Danny?"

He nodded his head. "I have to find out what happened. I blame this organization." He lowered his face and started to sob. "I should have paid more attention and joined her on retreat, before…" He lost it. I let him sob as I held his hand. Soon, we started to walk again … slowly, meditatively.

"How can I help you, Danny?" I whispered.

"What do you know about the members?" he asked.

"Um, very little. Bella is the only one I really know. And, I will admit my reason for coming here was because I was a little worried about her. She has a traumatic background and it would be easy for her to be brainwashed. So, yes, I guess I've been skeptical."

"So, you don't know the gurus?"

"No, not really."

"But, I saw you at their table so I wondered how you got that invite?"

I shrugged. I had no idea how we came to be sitting at their table the first night.

"Well, I sensed you were one of the good ones, Libby," he smiled and reminded me of my own father as he did. "How well do you know that famous techy guy?"

Famous? That was news to me. "Joseph Banter?"

"Yes. I don't trust that guy as far as I could throw him."

"He is sort of creepy, isn't he?" We both chuckled. "I

don't know. I can't figure him out. No, I don't trust him either. But, it's more in a way that he *always* seems to be hitting on the women."

Danny eyes narrowed. "Exactly."

"Had you met Bonnie yet?"

He shook his head. "No, but Katie had befriended her."

"You and Katie seem close."

"She reminds me of my daughter. After meeting her at the center in Mesa recently, we have met for coffee a couple times. I haven't revealed that Emily was once part of all this—no one knows that. Well, except you now. Our last names were different—divorce, you know—so I figured I could easily go undetected.

"Anyway, Katie wouldn't have met my Emily, since she'd only joined within the past year. But, she is so similar to my baby—I was immediately drawn to her. And, she's been nice to this old man, so we became friends. You know, I decided to join the retreat to learn more and try to protect her." He grinned.

"Makes sense. And, what have you learned?

He sighed. "Not much. Oh! But, I will warn … stop drinking the Kool-Aid, if you want to stay clear-eyed."

My head quickly turned to him. "What? Is that a metaphor? Or…"

He shook his head. Then I realized he meant it literally.

"The free freshly pressed juice? I love that stuff!"

We had reached the end of the labyrinth. He stopped walking and met my gaze again. "Just be careful, Libby."

I slowly nodded.

"And, stay away from Joseph."

We found our way back to the main intersection where

we each would go separately to our own quarters. "Danny, thanks for sharing with me. Let's keep all this between us. I'm not sure what's going on here, but I agree with you—and, I want to learn more about what happened to poor Bonnie, too. I hope it helps us learn more about Emily as well."

After a quick Namaste, we both ventured down our separate paths.

I'd rounded the corner where Joseph's cabin was and saw a girl who had walked out the front door. I popped behind the nearest tree. She was a tiny thing—black chin-length, bobbed hair, wearing a pink sari and flat sandals with leather straps that crisscrossed, winding up her legs. She walked in the opposite way and didn't appear to notice me. I course-corrected and decided to follow her from a distance. What I learned immediately was that she was a spritely one who was quick on her feet. I picked up my pace and found myself right in front of the guru's place. The cute woman was nowhere to be seen so I figured she must have gone inside. I wondered how one obtained an invitation to the seemingly sanctimonious palace? Did others just show up, knocking at the door?

I decided to try it. I boldly walked up the path, straight to the door, and used the giant door-knocker to announce my presence. I heard voices inside and footsteps were headed my direction. Panic began to set in. *What was my reason for being here?*

The door opened and Kali smiled broadly. "Libby! So nice to see you. Please, come in … leave your shoes here." She led me to a sitting room off the entryway. "What brings you to my place?"

That was exactly the answer I was still trying to come

up with. "Um. I wasn't sure if I should…" Quick thinking was something I was always good at—but today I was definitely stumbling. "It's just that…"

"It's okay, Libby. If everything isn't to your liking, I definitely need to know. What can we do for you to make your visit more enjoyable?" She signaled to a young woman standing outside the sitting room to bring us tea.

"Oh, no … I am enjoying myself immensely. You have beautiful grounds here and have thought of everything. I couldn't imagine a single thing that would…"

The tea arrived and was poured into cute little English teacups. Once the girl left the room, Kali closed the door so we could have some privacy.

"Okay. I feel uncomfortable saying this, but there is one guest I'm concerned about."

She looked at me worried. "A guest of ours?"

"Joseph Banter …"

She nodded her head, and left it slightly bowed as I continued.

"He has made me feel uncomfortable several times. Almost like he's following me. I've heard a couple other guests make similar remarks. 'Creepy' seems to be the term used most when describing him. I'm not sure what you can *do*, but I guess I'm asking about him because… well, should I have concern? He seems to know you both …"

"Libby, I can assure you we will deal with him. No, I don't know him well. He was sent here from his company's board…" she paused and reflected for a moment, "actually, it's not appropriate for me to discuss. Be assured, he won't be a problem any longer. Our guests' comfort is of the utmost importance, so I will investigate this. It won't be a problem."

My pulse quickened. *What have I done?* I mean, he was a creep and I don't like him much, but that doesn't mean he needed to get kicked out. And all because I'm nosy and wanted to see inside this place. I squirmed in my seat as I picked up my teacup and nervously took a sip.

"Thank you, Kali. I don't want to be a bother. Please ... maybe have a talk with him about personal space? I don't think he needs to be sent home or anything."

"Leave it to me." She finished her cup of tea and smiled. "Since you're here, let me show you around."

My spirit lightened. *Yes, exactly what I came for—I'd love to see the palace.*

I followed her out of the sitting room and down the hall. She explained that they host everyone from dignitaries to celebrities here. The place was decorated in colorful Indian tapestries, beautiful wall sconces, and statues throughout. I had been right before, there were two separate wings connected by a breezeway. She showed me to an enormous room that appeared to be set up as a ballroom. Staffers were buzzing about, cleaning. I kept looking for the girl that I had followed, but never ran into her. I also kept a lookout for staff members who resembled the group I'd seen come in here yesterday.

After the tour, Kali pleasantly asked if there was anything else she could do for me. I couldn't think of a single thing so I thanked her for her time. She walked me back to the front door and asked to be sure I'd join them for the activities today. After I affirmed I would, I walked through the doorway.

I'd made it down her front walkway when I saw Uma and the most divinely handsome man—I could only focus on his chiseled jawline outlined with five o'clock shadow.

She bowed slightly, giving a curious look that I took to mean *what are you doing here?* He flashed a brilliant white smile that nearly buckled my knees. I continued along after bowing to both of them and then did my best speed walk to get back to the other side of the compound again.

That's when I nearly ran headlong into him.

CHAPTER FIFTEEN

My stomach churned.

"What are you doing over here?" Joseph asked ominously.

Breathing heavily, I reached in my pocket for my notepad. I wrote: Just taking a nice meditative walk.

Ignoring all silent retreat protocol, he twisted his brows questioningly. He leaned in close and said aloud, "To me, it looks like you were running." His dark brown eyes glared, holding onto mine uncomfortably.

I backed away from him and began to walk away.

"Rude!" he yelled my direction.

I ran.

* * *

By the time I was back in our cabin, I realized I probably didn't have to run the whole way. It felt great though. Fresh air and getting away from a creep—very satisfying.

"Where have you been?" Bella inquired, suspiciously observing the sweat beading along my hairline.

"Nice day for a run. Oh, and Kali showed me around their place. Have you seen it? It's amazing."

"No, I've heard from others it's gorgeous, but I haven't been blessed yet."

Was that jealousy I detected? "Have you seen Katie since morning meditation? I was still concerned after she ran out of the chapel."

"No, uh, uh…" her eyes cast downward. "That's so sad about Bonnie, though, huh?"

"Has anyone said *how* she died? I mean, Katie said she was feeling ill, but I wonder…"

"I tried to ask around. Libby, everyone is acting so strange about it."

"How so?"

"Almost like they're afraid to speak."

"Because we're supposed to be in silence … or literally, they are afraid because of her death?"

She shrugged. "I've heard that several people have put in their request to leave early. I think people are afraid."

That was interesting and may explain why it seemed as though fewer people were around. It did make sense, I mean, I was uneasy due to Danny's story and his warning. I felt creeped out by Joseph. And, I wondered where Uma had been and why Lexi filled in for her. But, I hadn't felt the need to actually leave.

"How are *you* doing? Should we get in line for the next van?" I asked.

She laughed. "No! I'm having a great time. I mean, last night wasn't fun at all, but today I've never felt better. Sure, I'm concerned, but at the same time … she probably had a medical emergency and nothing anyone here could be responsible for."

I agreed with her, but decided not to fill her in on the several things I still questioned. "Have you found Jill?"

She looked deflated. "No. I guess she must have cancelled and really moved back to California. That's too bad."

It was time for the fire belly-breathing exercises with Uma, so we put on our yoga clothing and grabbed our gear to head back to the main building.

As soon as we walked in, I thought Bella had stopped breathing altogether. Her eyes were as huge as saucers and her mouth gaped open. I started to chuckle as soon as I saw who she was gawking at. The beautiful man I had seen with Uma earlier was stretching out on his mat at the front of the class. I noticed there were no men at this session yet, and every woman gravitated silently, right to the front of the room. Huge smiles were seen until they covered them with their masks. Bella and I were no different. While we waited for the class to start, I watched notes being exchanged between pairs of women at a furious rate. Giggles weren't being held back. I looked to the stage and saw the man was completely unaffected. He was probably used to women behaving like this in his presence. I sat there staring.

He was of average height and weight, muscles that bulged through his tight t-shirt, and his long dark brown hair lay in perfect curls right along his shoulder. He stood up and stretched his arms high above his head; every woman stopped and admired the six-pack abs when his shirt lifted slightly.

"Feel free to join me stretching whenever you are ready," he said casually.

In unison, everyone followed along, mimicking his stretches. I caught Bella's wink when I turned toward her. She was also admiring our newest session leader. The doors in the back of the room opened and Uma walked through. Once on stage with Mr. Handsome, she addressed the group while we watched him tie his gorgeous locks back into a ponytail.

"Welcome, my lovelies! And, it seems as though we're short some attendees today—guess they were unable to join us—that's a shame. Anyway, I am proud to introduce the one and only, Abram!" She took a step aside, as though we weren't already admiring the fine specimen.

Everyone clapped. Once the excitement died down, she continued, "All the way from Israel, he has come to join us at our retreat. He'll teach you all about the value of *breathing*. Yes, I know, I know … you *think* you know how to breathe, but put everything you know about it out of your head and be prepared to be wowed." She turned toward him and exclaimed, "Abram—they are all yours!"

Several gasps were heard and Uma joined in on the laughter that came next. There wasn't a woman in the room who didn't want to be *all his*.

Abram finally got the gaggle of women to settle down and then led us into breathing exercises. Throughout the session, it was hard to concentrate on breathing, but whatever his training was, he had certainly mastered it. By the time we were finished thirty minutes later, every participant was spent. We looked to one another as though we'd conquered Mt. Kilimanjaro or something.

On the way out, I overheard two women in front of us whisper, "I hear he is Uma's boyfriend…"

My notepad slipped out of my pocket and I knelt down to pick it up. When I stood, I realized Uma and Abram were right behind us. The fiery little red head and the breathing expert walked on around. They bowed to us, and continued down the walkway.

* * *

Shadow was more than ready for a walk when we got back to the cabin. I clipped on her leash and we headed for a part of the property I had been wanting to explore. On the way, I ran into Danny and gave him a nod with the tilt of my head, indicating he should join us. After petting Shadow, he nodded and followed. I could tell within a few feet down the path that he needed to talk. We wound along the pathways until we couldn't see or hear anyone.

"Did you see the guy with Uma earlier?" he whispered.

My eyes lifted. "Yes! He led the 'fire breathwork' today," I signed air quotes with one hand, "… just got back."

"Well, I remember Emily mentioning someone whom she described as looking exactly like him. She had told me she had fallen in love. He was from another country—"

"Israel?"

"Could be … I cannot remember the specifics. But, she was devastated when he returned to his homeland and she never heard from him again."

"And, you think this guest breathing expert is the same one she fell in love with?"

"Oh, I'm not sure about anything anymore, Libby. I know I could be grasping at straws. But, what *if* she did commit suicide because some man broke her heart?" Tears brimmed again, then he got serious. "I'll kill him!"

"No. Let's not go there, Danny. You said before—there's no way she could have committed suicide." I put a comforting hand on his back for a second, then sighed. "I truly hope you find the peace you'll need here to move forward from her death."

We walked in silence again until my attention was diverted as we came to a junction. Looking down the lane, the sign said 'Employees Only' but I wanted a peek. Danny got nervous and asked what I was doing.

"C'mon, let's go see…"

We continued down the graveled drive and after a bend in the road and rounding a clump of trees, there were several more dwellings. Shadow got excited and pulled to continue, but I held her back. We stood there observing, taking in the sights and sounds for a moment. One of the buildings appeared to be a maintenance shop—there were large tractors, a couple of pickup trucks with the Mercy logo on them. Beyond the shop, there were two buildings that could be housing. My guess was this would be where we'd find the staffers. After listening for a few minutes, we determined no one was around.

"C'mon, let's check this out."

"I don't know, Libby." Danny's fear was palpable.

I started to venture toward the maintenance shop. I wasn't sure what I'd use as an excuse if we were caught over here. For certain, I'd feign ignorance about the sign that was meant to keep us out. We peeked into the shop—there were several table saws, an array of shovels, rakes, and hoes. Everything that one would need to run an operation like this. Nothing strange about that.

Danny walked around the building on the outside. "Libby!" he hissed toward me.

He pointed at several vans parked behind the enormous metal shop. "Looks like the vans that brought us here, but no windows."

"Or Mercy logos…" I observed.

We continued our walk over to what appeared to be the residences. *Wonder who lived here? Staff? Maybe the girl I'd followed?* Curious whether anyone was around, I walked up to the door and knocked. Again, like earlier at the guru palace, I wasn't quite sure what to say if someone was here. Nothing like impromptu acting though. My heart beat a little faster. I swore I heard footsteps approaching. Shadow's ears perked curiously and her eyes went to the bottom of the door, then a slight tilt of her head. Someone was definitely in there.

Danny walked along the decking, looking in the windows. "Libby, we should probably go."

Out of the corner of my eye, I saw the curtain move. I knocked again. Shadow shuffled at my feet and continued to sniff the door frame, with her tail tucked and ears back.

"Hello!" I called out. This time Danny saw the curtains move too.

He backed off the patio, never taking his eyes off the window next to the door. "Libby. I don't think we're supposed to be here. I've got a bad feeling."

Once it was evident that no one would open the door, I pulled Shadow away and we followed Danny back down the graveled drive.

"Did you see the blonde who looked out the window?" he asked.

"I didn't see the actual person—only the curtain movement."

"Seems like someone is hiding out in there, doesn't it?"

Before I could answer, we both heard it. A vehicle had turned onto the drive. We scooted off into the overgrown bushes and trees to our right. I pulled Shadow in to me and held her tight, praying that she wouldn't bark. It was a white van driving slowly past us—no passenger windows, exactly like those by the shop. We watched as it pulled up to one of the residence cabins. A large man in uniform got out of the driver's seat and came around to open the sliding passenger door. Numerous young people with masks piled out of the van and followed single file onto the patio. I was startled by full face masks—like a ski mask, versus those we had been wearing for public health concerns. *Why would they wear ski masks?*

A tall blonde lady opened the door, and hurriedly shuffled them inside; they disappeared into the shadows. The blonde began speaking animatedly to the uniformed driver. She pointed our direction; he turned with a scowl on his face. She went back inside and closed the door.

Danny and I looked to each other, wondering which way to go. The man had climbed into the van and started it up. Before he had a chance to turn the vehicle around facing us, we hightailed it farther into the wilderness and away from the driveway.

Once we were far enough away and could no longer see the buildings, or the van on the road, we stood taller but continued to run. I had no idea which direction we were headed now or how we'd find our way back. It didn't matter, we needed to get as far away as possible from the road and that van. Eventually, we found another path and we decided to take it, slowing down to a casual walk—as though we had done nothing wrong.

"Do you suppose that's where the staff resides?" I

asked Danny.

"Is it normal to have staff in full face masks?"

"Wonder who that woman was? And, what did she say to that guy?"

"Yeah, I don't think this is good. We're easily identifiable, Libby." His eyes cast down to Shadow. My heart leapt.

"Well, what's our story when we're confronted about knocking at that door?"

"We got lost?" he suggested.

"Okay … we headed out on a walk, but couldn't find our way back. We were simply looking for directions."

"Libby—how did you know to go there?"

"My curiosity gets the best of me. I see 'do not enter' and it makes me want to enter." I sheepishly grinned as he shook his head at me.

We eventually found our way back to the labyrinth and from there, we knew where to go.

"Libby, should we say something—about those masked people?"

"I'm not sure we should. Not yet. I'm going to do some more investigating though. You don't need to be involved in this—don't worry."

"But, I am now anyway. Please, let me help you." He turned back in the direction we had come, and said, "Whatever that was, maybe it leads us to answers about Emily's death. Or Bonnie's."

"And Jill's disappearance…" I whispered, suddenly wondering if that was who was behind the curtains.

CHAPTER SIXTEEN

I found Bella curled up in a chair reading again when I got back to our place. She apparently sensed my energy. "Wow, you've been gone a while; guess Abram got your fire going," she teased.

I laughed, and then my voice turned serious. "Bella, do you have a picture of Jill?"

She set down her book and stood up. "What's wrong, Libby? Did you find her?"

"I may have seen someone matching the description. I would love to see a picture of her to be sure."

"If I did, it would be on my phone. And, obviously, we don't have phones with us so I cannot look." She moved by me to heat water for tea.

I completely forgot. There had to be a way to get to

those phones. Then I had a vision of the monstrosity guarding the compound.

"Where do you think you saw her? I've been looking everywhere since we've arrived here."

I didn't really want to divulge too much about what could only be the staff residence. I certainly didn't want Bella heading out on her own since I felt sure they'd be on guard now.

"Well, Danny, Shadow, and I were walking the pathways getting exercise. There was a tall girl with blonde hair. Guess that doesn't mean it's Jill—but, I did think of her."

"I think I know the one you're talking about. I've seen her a couple times myself and did a double take."

Deciding to change the conversation, I asked, "What teas did Badri drop off today?"

"I'm going to have one that says it's 'perfect energy'…" she held up the bag.

"Ok, I'll try that too."

"Sure you need any more energy?" she smiled.

Shadow was already lying down for a nap after our walk.

"I think I should try to rest for a while before our evening activities."

"Yeah, I'm a little nervous about what the 'fire' activity will be."

I grinned, kicking off my shoes. Shadow followed me into the bedroom where she plopped down on her bed in the corner. I closed the door and then started hunting for that envelope that Lexi had given me. It wasn't laying around, so I began searching drawers. When that didn't yield anything, I opened the closet, looked under the mattress—nothing. *Where did I put it?*

Bella tapped on my door. "Everything okay in there?"

I opened it up and let her in. "Have you seen an envelope laying around. White … with closures."

She turned back to the kitchen. "This?" She held it up and I grabbed it from her. "What is it?"

"Lexi handed this to me after last night's meditation. I think it's something from JJ but I'd completely forgotten after getting sick."

I tore into the envelope and there were several sheets of paper. He had handwritten on the top sheet: Call me later after you've read through. At first glance on the second sheet, I saw the Pima County Medical Examiner insignia at the top. As my eyes scanned the page, it detailed Bonnie's cause of death as asphyxiation, due to aspiration pneumonia. There was mention of a known epilepsy condition since childhood. I scanned the document further to see if a toxicity screening had been done; I found, 'pending'.

I sighed loudly, and Bella's eyebrows lifted questioningly, "What is this about?"

"Well, I'd asked JJ to look into cause of death for Bonnie. Katie was with her that night. Did you know that?"

She shook her head.

"She witnessed Bonnie's symptoms prior to her going unconscious. To me, it did sound a bit like a seizure. Although, she said she was complaining of a stomach ailment, too."

Bella interrupted, "Just like our sickness?"

"I'm not sure. We seemed to recover quickly. But, maybe it was, and in conjunction with Bonnie's pre-existing condition…" I flipped the page over and saw there were two more sheets of information, but not from the medical examiner. These looked to be printouts of online searches that JJ had done. They detailed several lawsuits filed against Love & Mercy.

"What … is there more?" Bella asked. I held up a finger as I continued to read through. My jaw dropped and I sat down on my disheveled bed. "Libby, you're scaring me."

"Well, looks like there are claims that L&M is masking itself as a religious organization, inappropriately taking federal tax exemptions." I skimmed further, then read, "Fraudulent financial practices. Apparently, there have been numerous other complaints. All within the past year."

"I had no idea. Do you think it's true? Or, maybe disgruntled members?"

I shrugged. How was I to know for sure?

Setting everything down next to me, I tried to quickly come up with next steps. *What did this have to do with Bonnie? Or whatever had scared Jill off? Were we in danger, having this knowledge?* Of course not. No one but JJ knew I had this information and they were only complaints—perhaps not even true.

"I'm sure there's a perfectly logical explanation. I can't imagine Kali would be involved in illegal activity. That is ridiculous." She began to pace the room. "But, where did Jill go? Why was there a hasty exit?"

"I wish I knew." And, I kept questioning whether I'd seen her earlier. *Why would she hide here? It couldn't have been her; doesn't make sense.*

"I'm struggling to make a connection that could tie Jill or Bonnie to Mercy's potential financial fraud." She kept pacing. "But we need to learn more. It's quite frightening to think L&M could be connected to either of those girls' situations. I don't know, do you think we should request to leave early?"

I couldn't imagine turning my back on these girls. Yes, we could be way off base … but to leave and not *try* to learn more while we're here. No, I couldn't leave.

"I'd understand if you wanna leave, Bella. But, honestly, we only have a couple more days … it's not that much longer before we'll be leaving anyway."

"True. And, we might learn more by staying."

"Exactly. My gut instinct says to stick it out and snoop some more."

"Then, I'd rather stay with you. I don't want to leave without you."

"Okay, then … we've gotta play it cool. Remember, we're here on retreat. We can't let anyone catch on that we're snooping around." Visions of Joseph potentially already on to me popped up. "I need to call JJ. Oh, and I believe that Danny is on our side, but other than that, let's be super careful." I shook the paperwork.

"Should we even share *anything* with Danny?" Bella asked

"He's here for a similar purpose so let's use that to our advantage." When questioned about Danny's purpose, I explained the story about his daughter. Bella looked heartbroken.

"However I can help, please … I really hope Danny's daughter wasn't part of any of it."

"Keep doing what you've been doing—get the most out of your retreat. If you can, keep your eyes and ears peeled."

We both went to our separate wings for the rest of the afternoon. I called JJ.

"What exactly do you think happened to Bonnie, if

not an epileptic seizure?" JJ asked me after we had talked through all the happenings since we arrived.

"Her friend indicated her stomach was bothering her. So, naturally, my mind moved toward poisoning. As you know, the report doesn't indicate that."

"Well, we still don't have the toxicology report back … the preliminary paperwork I sent to you was all I could get my hands on the other day."

"No news yet?"

"Not yet, but I'll follow up again."

"Thanks, JJ. Oh, and one more thing … Bella is concerned about a Jill Walsh. She seemingly has disappeared. I'm not sure what you could learn about her, but maybe…?"

"I'll see what I can do. I've got a full case load right now … but, I'll make a couple calls and let you know."

"I appreciate you, JJ. We have two more days, so I'm hoping to learn something more before we have to leave. I think I'll take Shadow for a walk before dinner … there's something about last night that hasn't set well with me. I need to ask some questions."

"Be careful, Libby." He hung up; my eyes followed my pup leaving the bedroom.

Shadow understood exactly what I meant when she'd heard her name. She jumped up from the floor and went straight over to the kitchen counter where I'd set her leash earlier. As I clipped it on, she bounced around eagerly.

We stepped out into the setting sun and walked around the guest residences. Shadow was on the trail of a squirrel who kept flirting with her and then would run up into a tree. It was everything I could do to keep hold of the leash as she pulled me to each tree and then bounced at the base while she looked up to the taunting rodent.

I heard voices coming from a nearby cabin, so I slowed, lingering and letting Shadow sniff around for her buddy. I couldn't make out whose voice I was hearing and had no idea whose little chalet we were near. We dawdled for several more minutes until I saw the door open and a man emerge. It was Abram.

He immediately saw Shadow and approached us. "Well, look at this nice pup," he said bending down to address her. "What's his name?"

My heart skipped a beat or two. He was the kind of man who makes a woman lose all her sensibilities, and his accent … I found myself catching my breath. *I'm not that kind of woman—focus, Libby!*

"Uh, *her* name is Shadow…"

"Aww, what a sweet girl." He looked up and I became more self-conscious. *What is wrong with me?* I prayed he hadn't noticed the flush that had spread over me. I hated how my pale skin got all splotchy when nervous. "Why don't you join Uma and me for dinner? I'm sure there's an extra spot at the table."

"Oh, uh … well, I'm here with my friend. Bella. So …"

"I'll let Uma know there'll be two at our table tonight then." With that, he turned and walked away.

I was left standing there, dumbfounded. I was pretty sure they rotated between guests being invited to the coveted guru table, and since we were there the first night, I wasn't sure that was possible. We'd see.

As my brain re-engaged, sending the signal to my feet to move again, I saw a tall blonde woman come out of the same cabin Abram had exited. She looked directly at me and then hurriedly walked away. We followed. Her pace was quite brisk, but we kept up. Finally, I said, "Excuse me!"

She turned abruptly and stared at me horrified. At least, that was my first impression; she had sunglasses on so I couldn't exactly see her eyes. I assumed her reaction was because I actually spoke out loud. Funny, I hadn't even questioned it when Abram came out of the cabin and talked to me. But, she was right—I shouldn't have yelled out like that. Shadow and I took another couple steps toward her.

"Hi! I was wondering…"

She bolted.

Shadow pulled and barked. I tried shushing her and we ran after the girl. She was too fast though and we lost her. I bent over with my hands resting on my knees, trying to catch my breath. Shadow wanted to continue—I'm sure she thought it was play time.

"No, girl. We lost her. Guess she didn't want to talk to us." I checked my watch; we had to get back.

* * *

Dressed in our finest—I wore a soft blue chiffon dress with a colorful butterfly pattern and Bella looked gorgeous in a dusty rose blouse and cream skirt—we made our way to the dining hall through the winding paths, and I quietly told her the story of running into Abram and then a blonde woman. I had no idea what Jill looked like, but again, I imagined this blonde could be her.

"Why would she run?" Bella asked.

"I don't know—but she seemed frightened by something."

"Maybe because you'd caught her with Uma's hot boyfriend?"

I laughed. "You could be right."

I couldn't help but think she went directly back to that place Danny and I shouldn't have been at earlier in the day. It was that direction she ran. I wasn't sure, but it could be the same person I saw. *Is that what frightened her?* I had Shadow with me then too—highly possible she recognized us. Goosebumps crawled up my arm.

We walked into the dining hall, looking around for familiar faces. Again, I couldn't help but wonder if the number of guests was dwindling. Maybe Bella was right— were people requesting to go home early after Bonnie's incident? Or, were more people falling ill? Where was everyone?

One of the waiters dressed in a tuxedo approached us.

"Ladies, right this way…" he led us directly to the guru table where Kali, Uma, and Abram were already sitting. Bella and I looked to one another nervously, but we followed and put on our best performance of the evening, as we put our palms together and bowed to each of them before taking our seats.

Abram spoke gently, muffled through his mask, "So happy you two could join us." He smiled broadly, nodding his head.

Kali gave him a slight admonishing look as she used her fingers in front of her lips to show 'quiet.' Personally, for once, I was thankful for the silence. I couldn't imagine what I would say and was slightly concerned I'd say too much.

From my seat, I saw Danny enter the room and shuffle off to a table two over from ours. His eyes were questioning mine. I gave him a slight nod. Katie was not with him, which concerned me. They'd been companions at most of the meals. I hadn't seen her since she ran out of meditation earlier. I used a similar questioning glance back at him. He shrugged his shoulders.

Bella observed the interaction; I held her gaze for a moment hoping somehow she'd pick up telepathically that I was concerned about Katie. I was not skilled at silently communicating.

When I looked back to our table companions, I saw everyone staring at us. *Great.* Then the tuxedoed man with the brilliant, perfectly coifed black hair, introduced two new guests to our table by pulling out their chairs and nodding around the table to the rest of us. The man I had seen in yoga class yesterday, but I'd never seen the young lady who was with him. I pulled my notepad out and wrote: Hi! I'm Libby. This is Bella.

As I handed it to him, I pointed between myself and my friend. He smiled. The lady with him was slight, maybe only five-two at most and extremely thin. She had black hair, deep dark eyes, and kept her gaze directly in front of her without looking at anyone. To me, she appeared uncomfortable at best. *I guess it would be uncomfortable—heck, I was too!* I tried to get her to look toward me, but it didn't work.

The distinguished looking gentleman wrote, I'm Ted Maizer—Senator from Ohio. He did not introduce his guest. She sat perfectly still and didn't attempt to introduce herself either. Bella and I nodded to him and, once he turned his attention to Kali, we stole a glance at each other. Bella agreed—weird situation. I commended myself for better telepathy that time. I'd seen him somewhere before, but couldn't imagine how it was I'd known a Senator from Ohio.

Within moments, the final seat at our table was filled

by Joseph. As Abram had, Joseph said collectively to the table, "Good evening, everyone!" Kali put her finger to her mouth. I could see that Joseph and Ted were familiar to each other and, of course, Bella and I were more than familiar with Mr. Slick. I noticed Kali gave me an empathetic look—she hadn't planned for him to sit at the table that night. That was clear.

I picked up my water glass and busied myself removing the mask to take a nice long drink. The second I placed the glass back onto the table, one of the tuxedoes appeared and my glass was filled again. I noticed tonight that there was no wine—I *really* wanted wine. My leg twitched—everything about me was uncomfortable; I was screaming inside to escape. Danny caught my eye from across the room—he understood.

Suddenly, the waiters all appeared with the dishes and set them down in front of each of us. Thank goodness I had something else to focus on. *What was it about Joseph that had me on edge?* When I looked back to him, he was sneering at me. *What's he looking at? Omigod! Could he read my mind?* I gave a little snicker back, but I'm sure my eyes sent daggers.

Most of us had finished eating, and the waiters had removed our plates. Kali stood, lifted a small spoon, and tapped it gently against her empty wine glass. All eyes in the already silent room shifted our way, gazing wondrously to the leader.

Softly, she gave us directions for our evening activity that would commence immediately following Satsang. She advised everyone to change from their evening wear into comfortable exercise clothing—but nothing loose or flowing and there was no need for footwear, so sandals were advised for walking to the chapel. We'd all meet there promptly at seven. With that, she slowly pushed her chair back, and seemingly floated from the room.

Uma and Abram glanced lovingly toward one another before he stood and held out his hand. She accepted it and slowly rose with his assistance. I felt like I was going to barf—it all felt so contrived and fairytale-like. She looked directly at me, picked up an envelope from near her place setting, and came around the table to my side. She bent over and quietly whispered in my ear, "hope to see you." I smiled, but I was baffled. *What was all this about?* Abram nodded his head and then the two disappeared into the exiting group.

Bella and I sat tight and I opened the envelope that was addressed only to me. Inside, I pulled out an elegant textured card etched with beautiful calligraphy. It read: Please join us tonight immediately following Satsang— Badri will be your driver. I sat staring at the filmy invitation, not knowing how to react. Danny touched my shoulder and I jumped, quickly folding the paper back into the envelope.

"Ready?" he said, looking around the now empty room, before asking, "May I escort you ladies back to your place?"

We accepted. The three of us walked quietly down the path and into our cabin. Once we were inside, Bella said, "What is that?" she pointed to the envelope I was still holding.

I pulled it out and let them read. I wasn't sure how to feel. My first reaction seemed to be fear. But this could also be a great way to see some of the inner workings—an invitation to a special event with the gurus. I felt sure this would get me back into the palace and perhaps I could do some snooping around.

Danny looked skeptical. "Libby, I'm not sure about this. Why only you and not with the *member* who invited you here?" he tilted his head toward Bella. Good question. I just shrugged my shoulders.

Bella piped up, "We'd better get changed for meditation. Are you going, Danny?"

He nodded and opened the door to leave. We had agreed to meet up again outside the chapel doors so we could find seats together.

* * *

Surprisingly, I found myself completely engaged in the meditation, after being so sure I wouldn't be able to shut down my brain. Once everyone opened their eyes again at the end, Uma explained the evening's 'fire' activity. Bella looked horrified. Danny was eager, and said he'd be Bella's partner. I realized that everything does happen for a reason and that invitation came at the perfect time. There was no part of me that wanted *anything* to do with walking through fire. I was now perfectly happy to attend the invitation-only gathering with the gurus.

We said our goodbyes outside of the chapel, where Badri was waiting for me with his golf cart. As he drove off, I looked back praying that my friend would be okay. What I should have been concerned about was my own safety instead.

CHAPTER SEVENTEEN

We wound through all the familiar paths I'd already explored, but when Badri went off road I became concerned. We drove for what seemed like twenty minutes through the dark. I noticed the trees became sparse, but the brush was severely overgrown on either side of the narrow trail. It was dark and I could only see the scanty path in the headlights ahead. The scrub brush made an eerie screeching sound along the cart as we passed. I pulled my arms and legs closer inside to prevent getting whipped.

"Badri. Where are we going?" I had envisioned we'd be going to the palace I'd visited earlier.

"Oh, missus. We go to the exclusive yurt."

"Uh, yurt? How far are we going? Seems as though we are really far from the resort now."

"No worries, Ms. Libby. You will love it here. So many stars…" he hummed as he continued to follow the tire tracks. I noticed large cottonwood trees appearing again. They seemed to thicken as we continued to drive. I wondered if this was near where the fresh spring was—there had to be water around for the trees to grow this thick.

Badri was lovely; we'd come to really enjoy his company. But, as we rode into the black darkness of night, I began to feel alone and isolated. I wished there were at least one other person on this cart with us. Safety in numbers, I suppose.

No sooner had I envisioned jumping off the cart and following the tracks back toward my cabin, I saw in the distance a beautiful golden glow. The yurt was enormous. Familiar with camping, I had pictured something slightly larger than a tent, but this was the size of an extensive home. As we turned off what I imagined had been a game trail, we proceeded up a well-graveled lane and right into a circular driveway. There were several other golf carts lined up at the base of a staircase, letting their passengers off. *Was I supposed to change into something nicer before coming here?* I breathed a sigh of relief when I realized that it was only the staff in suits. The attendees headed up the stairs were still wearing their yoga outfits from the earlier meditation session.

"Ok, Ms. Libby … I'll be waiting when you are ready."

I nearly said out loud 'I'm ready right now—take me back', but curiosity was getting the better of me now; I had to see inside this place. *Why are only some of us invited here? Why not everyone?*

"Thank you, Badri. I appreciate you bringing me all this way." I put my palms together, "Namaste." I scooted out of the cart and accepted a gentleman's hand up the stairway. Badri drove off.

It was breathtakingly serene the moment I stepped inside. The room was large with an elegant crystal chandelier casting the glow that I'd seen from afar. I was offered pink champagne—*now, this is more like it. Exactly what I wanted at dinner.* When I took a sip, I realized it was freshly squeezed juice and probably made fizzy with some club soda or something. It didn't exactly taste like champagne. Feeling now as though I had my social crutch—the wine glass—I started to walk the room more confidently. Everyone was talking; no silence at this party. Most were masked, unless sipping their juice. I realized my mask was down around my chin. I loved the juice and kept tipping my glass for more. Music and dancing as I'd seen in various Bollywood movies was pulling me in and I found myself tapping my foot with the rhythm.

"Good to see you here tonight, Libby." I startled, but managed to swallow the mouthful I had without spewing it everywhere. He had moved in close behind me, whispering in my ear. I turned abruptly, wide eyes, and ready to punch. It was Brian's handsome smile.

"Ugh. You've got to stop scaring me like that. I nearly swung—or, at best, you almost had drink all over you."

He started laughing. I could see he enjoyed my reaction. "What are you doing here? Where's Bella?" he asked.

"I was about to ask you the same—about being here. Bella didn't get an invitation."

He looked perplexed by that. "Hmm. But, she's the member."

"That's what I thought. I have no idea why I'm here. Do you know what this is all about?"

"Oh, they like to impress the newcomers. And we have several distinguished guests who arrived today." I remembered then that the Senator and his guest must be part of that entourage.

I looked down at what I was wearing … and saw that Brian was also in leisure wear. "Wouldn't they want it to be a dressy occasion then? Look at this place."

"Oh, *it is* a costume party…" As he said it, a couple pretty young ladies approached us.

"Ma'am, follow me." She took my hand and led me across the room, and I saw that Brian was being led in a different direction. We went down a hallway where there were multiple closed doors. She stopped in front of the one that said Shiva. "For tonight, you will be the goddess, Shiva. Please dress; leave your belongings in the room." I stared after her as she retreated.

My brain finally caught up with her instructions. "Wait! Is there a key to lock my belongings." I hadn't brought anything, but I wouldn't want my clothing walking away accidentally.

She shook her head and continued down the hallway.

I hesitantly opened the door. The room was dimly lit, but I could see a clothing rack and a beautiful floor-length mirror. Off to the side, there was a maroon old-fashioned velvet fainting sofa. I pulled the clothing from the hangers and held them out, admiring the bright colors and the softness of the silk sari. As I dressed, I wondered how they knew individual's clothing sizes, but once I figured out how the pieces fit together, I realized the loose-fitting outfit could be one-size-fits-all. I folded my clothes and set them on the settee and walked out of the room.

Back in the giant ballroom-like area, I grabbed another

glass from the waiter's tray. I looked around the room to find Brian, but didn't see him anywhere. In fact, the room was full of women—where had the men gone? It didn't matter. I found myself admiring the costumes—the full spectrum accented also by the sparkling light that bounced around from the chandelier. I felt more relaxed than I'd been in weeks. The music was thumping; my body had found the rhythm. Soon, I found myself immersed in the music, dancing the night away. One song after another; waiters passing by with trays of sweet treats and more juice; time evaporated.

Sweat dripped down the sides of my face when I decided to step off the dance floor, wondering where I'd find the ladies room. My body still thumping to the beat, I danced my way down the hallway. Many of the doors had names like, Lakshmi, Parvati, Durga, Devi, etc. I passed by my Shiva door. *Surely, there's a restroom somewhere close.*

I turned the knob on a door that didn't have a name. It was dark; I felt around inside on the wall for a switch. The second the light came on, I wished I'd never opened the door.

CHAPTER EIGHTEEN

W hat ... the..." I started.

Two young girls were huddled in a corner. After they blinked several times and rubbed their eyes, their look of terror was unmistakable. It was clear to me they weren't from around here, but I wasn't sure of their ethnicity. It was still quite dark even with the light on.

"Are you hiding?" I asked gently. They lowered their heads and would not look me in the eyes. I could see that they were scantily clad and a chill ran through me. Everything about the scenario felt wrong, and although I knew that, I was still having difficulty processing it. "Come out, let's go find help."

Their large brown eyes bulged; terrified. In broken English, one girl said, "No! No! Just leave. HURRY!"

Unsure what I should do, I simply followed orders. I turned off the light and as I shut the door, I told them not to worry—I'd be back shortly. I looked up and down the hall, but didn't find anyone. As I made it farther down the hall, opposite from the dancehall, I saw that it opened up into another fairly large room. Uma was standing at the threshold swaying to the music.

I tapped her on the shoulder with urgency. "Uma, there are some girls in trouble. I think they are hiding from someone. Come with me, I'll show you."

She slowly turned to me, smiling. "Good evening, Libby. Everyone is enjoying themselves this evening, don't you think?" Her seductive eyes gripped mine. "Go on, Libby … go enjoy yourself. I'll take care of everything." She all but pushed me into the room.

I could smell sandalwood incense; but I wasn't sure if that's what had created the fog disguising the people as ghostly images. Or was it a smoke machine for special effect? Through curtains of smoke, I could faintly see groups of people huddled in the corners. I thought I saw the distinguished gentleman from Ohio, but then a waiter popped out of nowhere, handing me a glass of juice and then disappearing back into the mist. Parched from dancing, I quickly consumed the pink liquid, but kept moving, hoping to make my way to the Senator, Brian, or someone I recognized who could help.

Where is the restroom? I should have asked Uma. Someone swept across my path, clearing more of the smoke away where I could see the 'bundles' of bodies. I squinted harder—*who are these people?* Some seemed familiar as I gazed off into the distance. *Was that the Senator I met earlier? I should go say hello now that we're allowed to talk.*

I jumped when an ominous voice whispered in my ear, "You don't belong here, Libby ... *leave. NOW!*" Whose voice was that? I spun around, but all I saw was an apparition seemingly floating away into denser fog. *Joseph?* I couldn't be sure.

I continued moving forward; my entire body feeling lighter and numb. Unable to see but a few inches in front of me, I ran into someone. A group of someone's actually. That's when I realized what was going on and I immediately bolted, shocked, but also laughing as I stumbled to get away. *What kind of party is this?*

My legs wobbled; I bounced into a wall, then struggled to steady myself. My eyes couldn't focus—I rubbed them, but everything blurred around me. I found the hallway that led me back to the dancehall. As I passed the room I'd entered earlier, I noticed the door was open. *Oh good, Uma must have helped them.*

So many beautiful ladies were still dancing—although now they appeared to me almost cartoon-like, anime characters everywhere morphing into ambidextrous positions. The lights strobed and bounced off every surface. I briefly held onto the wall for fear of falling. Sounds infiltrated my consciousness and vibrated throughout my body, energizing me. *I want to dance again!*

All fear melted away as I swayed over to my dancing partners from earlier, lifting my arms high into the air and twirling around and around. I felt like I could fly. Laughter and singing filled all my senses. Suddenly, someone wrapped their arms around my waist and lifted me high. *Wheee!* I *was* flying.

Coming back to earth, my legs were like gelatin; I crumpled into a heap onto the floor, laughing hysterically. I looked up and only saw legs all around me—colorful fabric swirled about. Then giant hands engulfed me; I cringed, but then accepted them. A blast of air hit my face, my hair fanned out, I was dancing again—flying around the room, my arms in the air like everyone else's.

"Lady…" I heard from the distance. I continued twirling only to come to an abrupt stop. "Hey … slow down."

Darkness filled the space behind my eyelids; warmth settled all around me. *Walking? Where was I going? But, I wanna dance!* Jiggly and limp; my body bounced around—*wait, someone was carrying me.* I moved my hand and reached up to their face. *Scratchy—ouch!* My hand fell, limply dangling. I heard music and laughing, but couldn't see a thing. My eyelids felt bulky and wouldn't budge as hard as I tried to pry them open.

That voice. I recognize the voice.

CHAPTER NINETEEN

A sunbeam pierced through a crack in the curtains and stabbed me in the eye. I turned away from the light, slowly rubbing and blinking several times. Shadow heard me stir and I felt her tail wagging, slicing the air with her tail. *Whoosh!*

Groggily, I reached out to her. "Hey girl." She started bouncing about and I tried to rise up to see her better. Instantly, the throbbing forced my head back to the pillow. "Ugh."

Bella slowly opened my door. "You alive in here?"

I turned to her with one eye open. "Ugh."

"Wow, you look like hell. Must have been *some party*." She laughed. "I'll go grab you some water."

My stomach churned at the thought. Shadow jumped

up on the bed and started licking my face. "No! Oh, sweet girl … give me a minute."

Bella walked back and set a water glass on the nightstand. "I'll take her out while you try to get going. We have yoga in about thirty minutes."

I stared at her blankly. "As if that's going to happen."

"I know, I know. Drink up … we'll be back in a few minutes."

After hearing the door close, I decided to try sitting up once again. I took a small sip of water when I discovered how thirsty I was. I ended up drinking the entire glass and wanting more. Slowly, I put my feet to the floor and tried standing.

Walking slowly to the kitchen, I started to remember how wobbly my legs were last night. I looked down and realized I only had a t-shirt on. I recalled something about beautiful colorful silk fabrics. I poured another glass of water and turned back to the bedroom. On the chair in there, the exercise clothes I wore yesterday were folded nice and tidy. I started to question memories of dancing in some costume. *How'd I get changed?* Nothing made sense.

Bella and Shadow bounded through the door. She saw I was standing. "Oh good, you *are* alive!" she giggled.

I smiled but struggled to remember details.

"I don't think I've ever seen you hung over before," she commented as she went about pouring some tea in a mug.

"You know, it doesn't exactly feel like a hangover necessarily." My brows furrowed. I took another long drink of water. I was already feeling much better. "Bella, I think I was drugged."

She abruptly looked up. "What? Why?"

We sat down on the sofa and I tried to recall the evening … from the time Badri picked me up outside the chapel to the last thing I remembered.

"I remember the euphoria of dancing. With a group of women. We were *free* and alive! I was having so much fun." Then a feeling came over me and suddenly I was self-conscious; butterflies in my stomach, and chills ran up my arms. I folded my arms around me and rocked slightly back and forth.

"What is it, Libby?" her voice was soft with concern.

"I remember a room—filled with smoke. It was like a haunted house with ghosts floating all about. Smelled sweet and woodsy at the same time." I accepted a mug of tea from Bella, and allowed the warmth to comfort me. "Bella, there were a lot of men in that room. At least the *forms* of men—it was difficult to see. Oh! And there were young women … I'd say girls because I cannot believe they were of age." In bits and pieces, images kept coming to me. I know I wasn't wearing my yoga outfit. I remembered smooth silky fabric against my skin. Then my eyes flew open, "OH! Oh, geez."

"What? What is it?"

"Two girls were in a small closet-like room. I thought it was the restroom until I turned on the light and I found them huddled up in the corner. I think they were hiding from someone…" I felt sick. I was supposed to have saved them. "I went looking for Brian…"

"Brian was there?" Bella seemed surprised.

"Yes. But, I only remember seeing him when I first arrived. After that, I don't remember seeing anyone I knew." I concentrated. I wanted to remember, but I was drawing a blank.

"Was this party at that 'palace' you described the other day?"

"No. Badri drove me somewhere really far away. You know what it was? It was a yurt."

"A yurt? As in, a *tent?*"

"Well, the exterior appeared to be. But, once I walked inside, I remember a fantastical ballroom. Waiters in full dress, everyone was *fancy*. I felt completely underdressed. That's when ..." The image was coming to me. A dressing room of sorts. "I changed into a sari in a small room. Then I looked like the other ladies there."

"Sounds beautiful."

"It really was." Again, chills took hold of me. I grabbed a blanket from the back of the couch and wrapped it around myself. "There's so much I don't remember. I have no recollection of changing back into my own clothing, for example. I don't remember coming home."

"Oh no, you were completely passed out cold when Badri carried you inside." Bella laughed. I gave her a surprised look. "He carried you to your room and then left. You wore the same clothes I saw you in during Satsang."

"Badri..." I couldn't remember seeing him after he dropped me off earlier in the evening.

"Yes. He was so sweet. Said something along the lines of 'Libby had too much fun.'" She giggled. "You don't remember any of that?"

Hmmm. My stomach churned with the knowledge that I had no memory.

"Bella, what time was that?"

"Oh, around 4 a.m. ... you literally partied all night long, girl!"

I ran for the bathroom as my stomach lurched. *What happened to me during all those hours?*

CHAPTER TWENTY

It was our last full day at the retreat, so once I had composed myself, I decided to join Bella for the morning yoga session. It would be outdoors and maybe fresh air was precisely what I needed. We didn't call Badri for a ride—I couldn't face him, and I needed to walk. Since it was the last day, I decided to bring Shadow along too. Everyone here had seemed to bond with her and what were they going to do, kick me out?

We arrived slightly early for the session and set our mats in the grass at the back, out of the way. Shadow began to roll around in the grass right next to me. Danny joined us shortly after, petting Shadow's belly as she sprawled out, loving every minute of it.

Uma's bright red hair caught my attention as she

walked by. She winked and gave me a mischievous grin. Goosebumps covered my arms. Soon after she walked by, so did Kali. No sign of the gorgeous Abram, and I didn't see Joseph anywhere. The second my thoughts went to Joseph, a sickening feeling swept over me again. Bella reached out and touched my arm, giving me the 'are you okay?' look silently. I took a couple deep breaths and nodded my head.

I felt better once we got into our yoga flow and I let my mind go. After finishing the session, everyone filed over to the dining room while I walked Shadow back to our place and poured her some kibble before I joined Bella and Danny for breakfast.

I stepped into the buffet line, grabbed some fruit and granola—not certain I could stomach anything more substantial. I passed on the juice altogether and poured some black tea instead. I sat down with Danny and Bella and slowly ate, and I was thankful for the silence.

Morning meditation further relaxed me and finally, I felt I could make it through the day without the need to scream … or run away. I left Danny and Bella outside of the chapel, while I took the long way back to the cabin.

I felt remarkably better and found myself wanting to run so I started out with a slight jog, and wound around the various paths enjoying the air coursing through my lungs, but feeling slightly guilty that I hadn't gone back and grabbed Shadow first. She would love this. Ah well, *my time*. And, I was loving it. To cool down from the run, I walked slowly through the labyrinth enjoying the nice overcast morning alone.

In the distance, I heard something and looked up from my meditative walk. Two people, through tall hedges near a cabin. I could see the upper bodies of a tall blond woman and a man with a ball cap on … wait, I squinted trying to focus in on the face. *Was it Joseph?* They were facing each other and apparently arguing. He grabbed her arm and she twisted from his grasp and turned to walk away. He yelled after her but she kept going. Seeing him looking all around, probably for witnesses, I knelt down pretending to tie my shoe, praying the hedge blocked his view. After a few seconds, I slowly stood, looking for him. I couldn't see him anywhere; he must have gone into that cabin. *Was his cabin this close to the labyrinth?* I didn't think so, but it wasn't the first time I'd found myself turned in circles.

I casually finished the walk through the labyrinth, taking an exit that I hadn't taken before. I looked around for familiar landmarks and saw the tip top of a metal roof, which I guessed was the maintenance building off in the distance. I chose to go left—away from the maintenance yard.

After walking past fields filled with sagebrush and cactus for ten minutes or so, I was getting quite warm. With no shade, the late morning sun beat down on my head. Checking my watch, something caught my eyes out in the field. A pile of dirt. *That's interesting.*

Curious, I carefully walked through the desert terrain, watching my step for critters, when I came upon several freshly dug holes in the ground. *What are these?* I stepped between the three unearthed rectangles—guessing that each was at least three feet wide and five to six feet deep. There were two-foot spaces between each of the cavities. Cautiously, I knelt down and took a handful of the fresh dirt, letting it gently sift through my fingers. It was moist. *This has been dug recently—very recently.* My heart skipped. My head lifted, eyes slowly scanning the area looking for any sign of life. Quail were running about, making their cute sounds. Other than that, no one was around. Still, I didn't feel safe. Everything in me said, *Run!* So, I did.

Back on the trail, I took off sprinting. Past the turnoff into the labyrinth on my right, eventually blowing by the Employees Only sign at the entrance to the maintenance yard. Along the way, I was passed by Uma and Abram in a golf cart. I gave them a quick wave, but didn't slow my pace. After another fifteen minutes, I finally saw the small community of cabins that looked like ours. I began to slow to a walk, breathless, and tired. Several members were casually walking about and I saw Danny and Bella were sitting quietly on our patio.

They were at the table with teacups and passing a notepad between them. I took a seat across from Danny. He pushed the notepad over, it read: Wow, that was quite a jog for someone who partied all night! I tilted my head and rolled my eyes with annoyance. Then I motioned, *let's go inside.* They understood and we all silently walked through the door.

As soon as it closed, I couldn't stop. I leaned over to pet my pup as the pent-up anxiety rolled from my mouth. I told them what I saw and approximately where I saw it. Shadow seemed to understand my unease, she sat on my foot, looking up at me with her ears back.

Bella, eyes wide, asked, "And, you think they are *graves?*"

Danny didn't know what to say. He stood shaking his head with clinched fists.

"What else could they be?" I had tried to come up with logical conclusions throughout the long run home. If the holes were meant for something like a trash burn pit, then why were they so perfectly rectangular and well, the size of the typical gravesite? Why else does one dig holes in the middle of the desert? All I could come up with was for hiding *something*. I prayed they weren't meant for *someone*.

Bella paced; Danny tossed out several thoughts, but in the end, we were stumped. Eventually, we changed the subject.

"Hey, remind me, what was the daily activity last night while I went to that party?" I asked.

"Fire walking … mind over matter. We walked across hot rocks barefoot," Danny grunted.

Right. Now I remembered, grimacing. "Did that hurt?"

"Not really. I went super-fast …" Bella added.

Danny shook his head no, also.

"Glad I missed that. But, I'm still questioning last night … I have few memories."

Danny's head whipped around to me. "Yeah, where did you go?"

The three of us took seats and I told him what I remembered about the night before. I had calmed down since Bella confirmed that Badri had brought me home. Prior to learning that, I felt so unsettled. I still hadn't remembered dressing myself into my own clothes, so that question still lingered as well.

"Was our favorite tech guy at the party?" Bella asked.

I searched the memory bank, but never recalled seeing him. I shook my head. "I also didn't see Brian after we first arrived at the yurt. I wonder where he went off to?" My eyes went skyward as though I expected the answers to come from the ceiling.

Bella turned to Danny. "Hey, Katie wasn't at yoga, breakfast, or meditation this morning. Have you seen her?

Is she okay?"

"I haven't heard from her at all. I did knock on her door before heading over to yoga. She didn't answer."

I had forgotten we hadn't heard from her for a full day now. "Let's go over there ... that concerns me. The last I saw her, she was so upset about Bonnie's death."

I reached for Shadow's leash and the others put their teacups in the sink. We set off down the trail to Katie's place. As we stepped up to the door, I listened for sounds. It seemed dark and quiet in the windows. Danny knocked loudly. After a few more seconds, all three of us knocked and yelled out her name.

"Guys, there are no locks." I grabbed the doorknob and turned it. "Katie? Are you here?" I yelled as we stepped over the threshold.

Everything was tidy. The kitchen and living areas were clean, no personal belongings laying around. We rounded the corner to the only bedroom. "Katie..." There was no answer so I proceeded. The bed was made and no sign of anyone. I opened the drawers and closet—nothing. None of her belongings were anywhere in the cabin. It appeared as though she must have checked out and gone home.

Danny pulled a phone out of his pocket. Bella and I gave him a look.

"I know, I know ... sue me." He punched a button on the prohibited device, held it to his ear, and waited. After a few seconds, he said, "Katie, it's Danny. We're worried about you. Please call me as soon as you get the message." He punched another button and put the phone back in his pocket.

"Libby also snuck her phone in." Bella divulged.

I gave a sheepish look as Danny returned a wide smile.

"I knew I'd like you from the moment we met, Libby Madsen." He laughed and gave me a hug. Bella looked at both of us as the delinquents we were.

"Well, let's get out of here. Should we ask Kali the whereabouts of our friend?" Bella asked.

We all agreed it was worth a try. I showed them the way to the guru's residence and they were equally mesmerized at the beauty of the gardens as well as the palace. It was quite the elaborate setup, which I admired again, as we walked up the path to the door. We knocked and a young man answered.

"Yes. Can I help you?" he asked, a bit pompously, I thought.

Bella sweetly spoke up. "Could we speak to Kali, please?"

At first, I thought he was going to reject our request, but then the tall Indian goddess-like figure walked up from behind him. "I'll take this, Joe," she calmly said. The sunshine hit her silver hair as she stepped into the doorway.

Looking jilted, the doorman walked away. Kali smiled broadly, "Libby! Good to see you again," she winked at me, chuckling. Then, "Bella, Danny, do come in." We passed a diminutive young lady who stood stiffly at the doorway. She looked familiar. Her uniform was a crisp white linen shirt and a green plaid skirt. She almost looked like a mannequin; only her eyes moved as we passed, otherwise she remained gazing straight ahead. I realized I was staring, perhaps making her uncomfortable. *Did she shake her head?* I wondered as Kali led us through to the familiar sitting room and asked us to take a seat. *Did I know this girl?*

Bella was quick to get to the point of our visit once we took seats on the sofa. "We were wondering if Katie

Sanchez was alright? It appears she's left and we're concerned."

Kali's eyes looked toward her hands which were crossed in her lap. "I'm afraid she has left the retreat." She looked up at us, frowning slightly.

"Can you tell us why? It's unlike her to not have told us she was leaving..." I asked.

"I'm sorry. The privacy of our members is of utmost importance to us." There was irritation in her dismissive response. She called out to the girl outside the door, "Tea, please." The young lady quickly moved from her position and was back within moments with a full tea service. She set the tray down in the middle of the coffee table, and I noticed her shaking as she poured. I figured the poor girl must have been new at this; she seemed unsure of herself. I wanted to reach out and help, but figured that could make things more difficult. She carefully picked up one of the delicate teacups, sloshing the hot liquid over onto its saucer, and offered it to Danny. Slowly, she continued as each of us accepted her offering. I felt the tension— apparently, even gurus get impatient sometimes.

As we each doctored our tea to our liking, Kali silently kept her eyes on each of us. I hadn't been uncomfortable in her presence before, but now I felt the need to get out. I smiled at her, then looked down. I couldn't help but notice there was something about the girl who had just brought us tea. *Where had I seen her before?*

Finally, Bella changed subjects, and asked about the plan for the rest of the day. We had the schedule, so I knew my friend was filling the void, she being equally uneasy. Kali indulged us and reminded that today was an 'earth' focus. In the afternoon, we'd plant some trees and flowers and then there was a surprise group trust activity planned tonight.

Danny and I must have had the same thought—our eyes met guardedly.

Earth ... *graves?*

CHAPTER TWENTY-ONE

As we walked back toward the main buildings, Danny finally broke our concentration and whispered, "Is anyone else worried about tonight's activity?"

Bella and I nodded. Shadow let out a woof.

We passed several people who had glazed smiles plastered on their faces. That brought me back to what Danny mentioned before about the juice shots given before every session or activity. *Was I drugged by that delicious juice last night?* I wasn't sure if that was it, or maybe it was alcoholic and I simply got drunk. Since I'd only ever been what I considered to be *drunk* maybe a couple times *ever,* I was skeptical. Not once had I lost memory before, or had passed out from drinking, though. Last night felt different. I agreed with Danny's warning now. No more juice.

As soon as we were in the sanctity of our own walls, Bella sat on the sofa, letting out a *hmmph* and shaking her head.

"Do you buy, for even one second, that Katie *chose* to leave?" she questioned.

Danny twisted in his seat to answer. "Not really. But, on the other hand, she was quite upset over Bonnie so I suppose it's not *that* unreasonable to consider."

"I don't know. Something is fishy and I don't like it."

"Did you happen to notice the girl who served us tea? How nervous she was?" I asked.

She shook her head. "Uh-uh. Well, I mean, yes, I saw how she nearly dumped hot tea onto Danny." We all chuckled, remembering. "But, I can't even tell you what she looked like—I wasn't that focused on her."

Danny stood up. "Ladies, I'm far more concerned about the graves Libby found than the girl who served us tea." He looked over to me. "Wanna show us this place?"

Shadow barked, staring up at me with a look that I took to mean, *please*. I was unsure if we should go over there again, but it would help to have witnesses. What if I was still under the influence—what if nothing was as it seemed? To prove to myself that I wasn't going crazy, I gave in and we headed out the door again.

* * *

"They should be seen when we round the next curve in the trail." Shadow was pulling with all her might and I tried to hold onto her. "Calm down, girl."

Danny turned around looking at where we'd come from. "This is really far from camp."

"You think this is far? Should have seen where Badri

drove me last night." That got me wondering if I could ever find that place again. *Which direction had we gone? Was I already 'juiced' before I ever got into his cart?*

Bella got excited. "Is that it over there?" she pointed to a heap of dirt.

I nodded my head and stepped off the trail to cross the desert toward the pile. Shadow yanked and I dropped the leash. She was probably okay this far away from everyone; she wouldn't bother anything. As I examined the fresh dirt, I wasn't sure if my memory was failing me, or were the holes deeper now. *Had someone been here since I was?*

"Sure looks like a grave," Danny's voice was quiet and somber as he lowered his head. I hadn't considered the weight of this for him.

"Wonder what has her all wound up?" Bella noticed. Shadow's nose was in overdrive. Winding her way around each hole, she was running back and forth, whining.

Dirt started to fly. By the time I got to her side, Shadow already had a good size hole going and showed no signs of stopping. "Shadow! Stop it!" I said, trying to grab for her harness. She never acknowledged me at all. Then, she nosed her way into the fresh dirt, and came out shaking all of it off.

Danny pointed. "What's in her mouth?"

I grabbed her and made her sit. Fishing through her mouth, I pulled out a slobbery string-like thing. Once I wiped it off, it looked like a homemade friendship bracelet that young girls loved creating. There were strands of yarn, or heavyweight string, braided together with colorful beads. In the middle of the circular bracelet was a metallic infinity symbol. As small as it was, it would only fit a tiny wrist.

I shoved it in my pocket and reached down to pull Shadow back. Her nose was buried halfway up her snout, going after something else. I knelt down and gently pushed her aside. Bella and Danny joined me and we combed through the dirt, looking for ... what? ... I wasn't sure. Shadow whined insistently.

"Here's something," Danny pulled up a long strand of beads. "Mala ... why would prayer beads be buried in the dirt?"

We all whipped our heads around when we heard Brian's voice. Shadow ran over to her buddy with full gusto.

"What are you guys doing out here?" his voice had an edge to it I hadn't witnessed before. He reached down and quickly petted Shadow.

"Hi! What are *you* doing out here?" I tried to tease, but his face remained sober. I stood up and walked over to him. "Uh, yeah, we were on a walk ... Shadow got interested in something over here. Musta thought they needed help digging holes." I laughed.

"Y'all better get back..." he pointed down the lane where we'd come from.

"Hey, why do you think they're digging out here anyway ... those are some awfully big holes, don't you think?" I watched Brian's face as he looked over where my friends were still sifting through dirt.

"What are they looking for?" he asked, without addressing my question.

"Oh, we were wondering what Shadow was so intent on. Nothing there though."

"Well, really, Libby. You guys should get out of here."

"Okay. No problem. Just enjoying the lovely day." I didn't like how serious he had become. "Hey, where'd you run off to last night anyway? I was hoping to have a dance partner."

"Libby ..." he started to say, then turned to Danny and

Bella as they walked up.

My eyebrows lifted in question. "You were saying?"

"Oh nothing. But, I'll see you later tonight." He set off, continuing farther down the path. Not the direction toward the residences and the main buildings. I watched until I couldn't see him any longer.

Bella noticed it. "I don't think I've ever seen him *not smiling*. What was wrong?"

I shook my head—I had no idea. But I sure wanted to know what was down that direction Brian went. I might need to check it out later.

* * *

After Danny left our place, I dug the bracelet from my pocket, setting it on my nightstand. We still had several hours before dinner and the evening's activities. I grabbed my phone from underneath the mattress and turned it on.

Bella was in the shower, so I decided to call JJ instead of going back and forth with text messages. Listening to it ring, I prayed he'd answer.

"Hey Libby!" his friendly voice rang out.

"JJ—so happy you answered. Hey, I need more favors…"

"Whatcha need?"

I filled him in on what Danny told me about his daughter, Emily. Asked him to see what he could learn about Katerina Sanchez from Brooklyn—had she indeed made it home? If I could only get a phone number for her, I'd call her myself. I also related the events from last night about potentially being drugged, finding those girls hiding, and the crazy party room. Had there been complaints about drugs, or maybe sex parties, as part of these retreats previously? I was curious about any information on Senator Maizer—was he on the Love & Mercy Board of Directors?

"You really think all that's going on down there, huh?" he asked. "And, you suspect a senator is somehow involved in illegal activities?"

"Honestly, I'm not sure of anything except that Bella is worried about Jill's whereabouts and her mental state. Bonnie died here. And, supposedly Katie has left early—but did she really?" I sighed. "Maybe it's nothing, and maybe these are all circumstantial situations that only seem weird to me. However, one thing I haven't told you yet—we found three freshly dug holes out in the desert on the L&M property."

"What does that mean?"

"JJ—they are large enough to be graves."

He promised to do some research and I told him I'd call him back before the evening activities. Before I turned my phone off, I checked for messages from Greg. There were none. I quickly texted telling him how much I missed him. My heart hurt as I longed to hear his comforting voice. I let him know we'd be home tomorrow evening and I'd call then.

Once I'd turned off my phone and hid it again, I decided to sneak out before Bella could question where we were going. I quickly leashed Shadow and off we went again.

* * *

We followed the path from earlier, back around by the freshly dug mounds of dirt, farther down the path until

I recognized it. This was the small trail that Badri had ventured off when he took me to the yurt. In the dark, it seemed we'd driven forever, but I was curious now to see this in daylight.

Shadow disappeared within the brush; I estimated it to be nearly my height. I held onto the leash for fear that if she actually got away, I might never find her again. After fighting off the desert brush for what felt like hours, I looked at my watch. We'd only been on the trail for forty-five minutes. Up ahead, I could see that there was a break in the scrub. Shadow was anxious to keep going so I let her pull me along. When we worked our way out of the brush and into the open, I suddenly felt vulnerable. At least in the brush, we were mostly hidden; now we were exposed. Quickly scanning the area, I saw a cluster of cottonwood trees not far away. We were close. We stopped and I reached for the water bottle I'd stashed in my pack. I knelt down, cupping my hand and poured water into it. Shadow lapped it up.

"C'mon, girl. Over there." I pointed slightly to our left and we headed toward the cluster of trees. As we came closer, I could confirm that this is where I'd been for that party. The yurt was huge, but in the daylight, it didn't appear as magical. I could see several golf carts parked around, but so far, couldn't see any people. We moved to be within the trees and I knelt down to Shadow's level. Her tongue was hanging out panting, thankful for the break. My eyes swept left and right, searching the area. The main entrance doors were open and when I squinted, I could barely make out figures moving about inside. A man stepped outside— the senator; I was sure of it. I stayed in a squatted position, rubbing Shadow and praying she wouldn't move. Even though we were at least fifty yards away, I didn't want to have to explain what we were doing here. Movement caught my attention again. A young woman stepped out, took the senator by the hand, and they disappeared into the darkness beyond the threshold.

"Let's try to get closer, girl…" I stood, slightly crouched, and we moved within the trees until we were close to one side of the structure. There were no windows on this side. I looked around for people and then we continued around to the back. I knew there was another door somewhere at that end of the monstrosity of a tent. What I didn't know was that there were multiple outbuildings that couldn't be seen from the front driveway. Small houses, it looked like. I pulled Shadow closer to me and we hid behind a large shrub beside the first structure we came upon. Someone was exiting the back of the yurt.

"Shhhhh…" I stroked Shadow's fur, keeping her calm.

Uma led a suit-clad gentleman out of the tent structure and pointed to her right. Thankfully, their concentration was focused away from us. He headed off in the opposite direction from us, as we continued to crouch behind a building close by. I could see him walk up to the door of one of the residences. She stood soaking in the sunshine; eyes closed and head tilted to the sun. Kali came out behind her. I'd never seen Kali look upset since I'd met her, but now, I could tell she was not a happy camper. Uma's arms flailed about and she pointed in the direction she'd sent the man. I wanted to be closer where I could better hear the conversation, but didn't dare budge for fear of being discovered.

"You have no idea…" Uma shouted.

"Fill me in then, please," Kali grimaced.

Electricity filled the air; I could feel the tension between those two from my hiding spot. Uma gesticulating with her hands. Kali's face contorted and her hands went to her hips. Shadow finally realized what I was doing and her ears perked up. I shushed again, and kept petting. I really wish I could hear the whole conversation. What were they so upset about on retreat? Clearly, it had something to do with the man that Uma was with.

They turned and walked inside. Once I was sure no one else was walking out, I led Shadow around the back of the house we'd huddled near. I looked in the windows as I passed, trying to determine if they were occupied. Curtains covered every window, so we stayed quiet in case someone was in there. On the other side of the house, there was a large pile of wood. From there, I could see directly into the yurt; Kali and Uma were still standing inside the entrance and Uma looked pissed.

"Get him out of here now!" Kali screamed. "You know how I feel. Now, get it done."

Uma stormed out the doorway, down the steps, and marched right over to the building where she'd sent that man. Shadow stood and shook—I held on to her tags. "Shhhhh … Shadow. You're going to get us in trouble." Neither guru noticed us. I sunk down lower as Uma stomped on by.

"C'mon, Shadow … let's go." We crept around the back of the buildings and made our way closer to the one where Uma headed. I prayed no one was paying attention as we lurked around trying to go unnoticed.

A door slammed. My heart leapt as I peeked around the side of the house. Uma was climbing the steps back into yurt. *Who was the man she'd sent to this cabin, and was he who*

Kali wanted out? Clearly, there was dissention in the ranks; now I needed to figure why.

My head whipped around at the sound of leaves crunching behind me. Shadow barked and that's when the dark-clothed man turned toward us. I fiddled with my shoelaces as my excuse, and pulled Shadow closer to me. Carefully looking up through my eyelashes, I saw Brian's wide smile. Shadow wiggled uncontrollably as he approached us. As I stood up, a huge sigh of relief washed over me.

"Hey, Libby! Whatcha doing over here?" he yelled out, much louder than I would have preferred. I mean, weren't we still supposed to be silent?

"Oh, out getting the pup some exercise. Beautiful day!" I said quieter, as I noticed he glanced at the cabin we'd been crouched next to. I pointed to my feet. "Stepped off trail to tie the laces…" I shrugged.

"Yes, it's gorgeous out. Listen, I have to drop something off with Kali…" he shook a cellphone he had in his hand. "After that, wanna grab a juice with me? It's a great afternoon for soaking up the sun by the pool." His eyebrows lifted encouragingly. His anxiety from earlier had completely disappeared. This was the good ol' Brian I knew.

"Sure. Sounds good. I'll take Shadow back and meet you at the juice bar in what, an hour?" It would be good to talk to a friend, I had decided, even though there was no way I was touching the juice. He agreed with the time as he turned toward the yurt and bounded up the steps. I turned to leave down the path, in time to see Joseph coming out of a cabin.

CHAPTER TWENTY-TWO

Shadow and I picked up the pace home. My heart thumped uncontrollably after avoiding the creepy guy. What was it about him? Every nerve responded, and not in a good way either. I noticed Shadow was extra edgy as well. We pushed forward at a fast clip until we bounded up the steps to our cabin.

Shadow hurried to the water bowl. Bella was nowhere around and I quickly freshened up to meet Brian. It had been good to see that his mood had changed. I filled my water bottle and realized my spirit had picked up from earlier; I was actually excited to spend time with him again. Plus, maybe he could shed some light on what he was so upset about before.

"Shadow—on your bed. Here are a couple cookies till

I return; I'll be right back," I cooed to her as I kissed her forehead. I looked around for my keys, then remembered I didn't have any. "You protect our place, ok?" Her head fell and she was snoozing before I could reach the door.

* * *

My skin tingled and I noticed the goosebumps forming. I'd watched Brian jog the final hundred feet to where I was sitting outside the juice bar. The attractive ginger-headed man was difficult not to notice.

"Sorry, that took longer than I'd thought. I should have taken a golf cart back." I smiled at him, then remembered I hadn't seen Badri for most of the day. I needed to thank him for bringing me home the night before. "Did you get juice?" he asked, pointing at my water container.

"I'm good for right now. Need to drink water for awhile." I picked my jug up and took a sip. He ran off to fetch his drink and was back in remarkable time.

"You sure?" he held out his cup. "Pineapple, kale, wheat grass, and cucumber..." His eyes sparkled as he tried to sell me on a sip.

I laughed. "No thank you, maybe later." I stood and we slowly walked the path, crossing the bridge overlooking the lazy river, and then over to the pool and spa area.

"Have you gotten a massage here yet?"

"You know, I hadn't even thought about it, but probably should."

"They are ah-maz-ing!" his eyes rolled back into his head.

"So, where did you run off to last night? You never came back to dance with me?" The images of lights, smoke, and moving bodies came back to me.

"Oh, after they tried to dress me in one of those getups, I wriggled my way out and called it a night." He shrugged, and his eyes met mine. "I wasn't sure what kind of party it was, but figured out pretty quickly it wasn't my kind."

I remembered walking through the smoke-filled room. I could have sworn I'd seen Brian from far away, but then again, everything was so muddled. There wasn't much I could remember, even now.

We quietly walked through the pool fence gate and chose a couple chaise lounges to sit on. Looking around, silver hair caught my attention.

"Hey, Brian," I whispered and nudged him, his head snapped my direction. "Don't look now, but do you know that guy who is in the hot tub?"

He stood, shook out his towel and turned to lay it out on the chair while glancing toward the gazebo where the hot tub was. After repositioning himself to lie down, he casually turned his head. "Senator Maizer … yep. He's one of the many guests they are hosting this week. Why?"

"He's very handsome…"

"Libby! You are taken!" he teased me.

"I know, but that doesn't mean I can't admire a good looking man!" I took a sip of water, then turned to Brian. "I saw him earlier, over in that yurt community."

"Yurt community?" he busted out laughing.

"Well, do you have a better name for it?"

He stopped to think for a moment. "Uh, no. I can't remember what they call it, but it's where they host large events. They always seem to house special guests over there too."

"I thought *we* were pretty special."

"Of course, we are! That's probably why we were

invited to their party last night."

"I was wondering why some of us meditators were invited while others weren't."

"What do you think of the place so far?" he asked, ignoring my previous statement. "Think you'll become a member?"

I thought about the question for a second, then approached cautiously, wondering what his experience has been. "I'm thinking about it. What exactly is involved in being a member?"

"Well, you get to come to these special events, for one," he started counting off using his fingers. "There are *many* self-help courses—they're great! I love the fellowship and networking opportunities as well as exploring my spirituality more in depth."

"I hear it's really pricey."

He sat up and turned toward me, elbows on his knees. "So are psychologists and college teachers. I've learned more here than in any school I've attended. It's worth it—trust me."

"I've heard of levels you have to achieve. What level are you at—and why is that important?"

"Oh, yes. I'm still working my way through—so I'm only at bronze level. It's the path to enlightenment. After passing different courses and achieving milestones, you'll ultimately reach the blue diamond level. You can't be a guru until you've achieved that—so that's my goal. I want to be the next highly sought-after guru!"

That surprised me. In all the lunch and dinner conversations that Brian and I had back home over the past couple months, this was new information.

"How much have you already spent getting to a bronze

level?" I ventured.

"That doesn't matter, Libby. What matters is doing the work to improve your mindset—your outlook in life." He reached down to pick up his juice and took a sip. "Take care of yourself and make that the most important thing you can do to reach your goals."

Now he was sounding like an advertisement. I shook my head, laughing.

"No, really, Libby. You should consider it. I can sponsor you—or, of course, Bella could."

"Yeah, and who's going to pay the bills? I can't afford this," I swept my arms out, looking at their facilities. "And, I don't understand how you and Bella can. We all work in the same place!"

He laid back down on the lounge chair and was quiet for several minutes before adding, "When you're interested, let me know. For now, let's get the last of the sun before we have to dress for dinner."

"I'm nervous about tonight's event. Do you know what the earth element is all about?"

He shook his head, but the look I saw in his eyes had me wondering. There was something he wasn't saying.

"Did you know Bonnie? Or Katie?"

"Who?" he turned his head quickly.

"Bonnie was the girl who died—they mentioned to all of us. Katie was a guest, but I guess she's gone home. I'm worried about her."

"Why?"

"Well, from what I understand from her friend, she was quite upset after Bonnie's death. We didn't know she was thinking of going home, but then suddenly her place is cleared out. They said she'd left early."

Tension filled the air. He sat up and pulled the towel that had wadded up underneath him. "Why would I know these girls?" he spat, clearly upset.

"Whoa! I was just asking a question. They're members, so I thought…" I held my hands up in defense as he abruptly stood. "Sheesh!"

His eyebrows were still knitted together as he turned to me. "I've gotta go get cleaned up. See you later."

Confused, I nodded and gave him a little wave goodbye. What exactly had I said to set him off? I gathered my towel and deposited it in the marked basket on the way out. He was long gone and I set off at a quick clip back to the cabin. I'd never seen Brian so angry—he'd always been so amiable.

Bella wasn't there when I returned; I decided to take a shower and rest before dressing for the evening events. First, maybe JJ had learned more. I lifted the edge of the mattress, reaching my hand under to retrieve my phone. Feeling around in a wide arc, I didn't feel it. I lifted the mattress higher up and looked under—nothing. Frantically, I tipped it all the way over and began rifling through the covers too. *I know I put it back here!* My eyes scanned the room. *Had I left it out somewhere?* Desperate, I began opening drawers, gutting the insides until all my clothing was strewn across the floor—nothing!

I ran through the cabin ripping cushions from the sofa, reaching under furniture, and rummaging through drawers in the kitchen and bathroom. I glanced in Bella's room and decided I shouldn't go through her stuff. I'd ask her when she returned. Standing still in the middle of the room, I found myself staring at the door handle; chills ran up my spine. *Someone had been in here—someone robbed me!*

I paced quickly, back and forth. I hadn't noticed anything disturbed when I walked in, so someone knew what they were looking for and where to look. *How?* Then the image of Joseph popped in my brain. The first day we were here, I'd nearly forgotten—*he saw me taking pictures! He knew about the phone!*

Looking at the clock, I knew I needed to get ready for the evening's activities. I showered, but my mind raced the entire time …what would *he* want with my phone? I struggled to remember the content of the photos I'd taken. So much had happened since then, and as I recalled they were fairly innocuous—scenery, not much more.

I was drying off when I heard the door open.

"Are you here, Libby?" Bella called out. "Shadow and I went for a walk—we're back!"

"Out in a minute…" I quickly dressed and then opened the bathroom door. I heard Shadow lapping up water and then smiled as she plopped down onto the wooden flooring, panting heavily. "Hey, did you get my phone from under the mattress?"

Her look of confusion answered my question. *Shit!*

"That means that someone broke in while you were gone. When did you and Shadow leave?"

Her eyes widened. "When was the last time you used your phone?" she asked in return, as her eyes scanned the room.

Good point. *Had it been a couple days already?* No. *Was that really only yesterday? Feels like we've been here weeks.* "I'm pretty sure I texted Greg and JJ yesterday afternoon."

"Well, there have been a number of times since then that both of us have been gone. Don't know how we can pinpoint it to this afternoon." She walked to my bedroom, peering around the doorframe. Looking horrified, she spun around, "Is this how they left your room?"

"I did that ... looking for it." I sighed. She was right; someone could have grabbed it at any time we were away. "Who do I report this to?"

"Really? You want to admit you snuck in the phone?"

"Yes! I know, I know ... I'll fall on my sword and admit I broke rules, but someone *stole* from me and I want my phone back!"

"I suppose we could tell Badri and he'd get the ball rolling to help us?"

I agreed.

When Badri arrived, I first thanked him for driving me home the night before. I had many more questions for him, but hoped we'd find more time alone, later. Then I brought up my phone. After enduring an animated lecture, of which most I couldn't understand, he agreed to help me find it.

CHAPTER TWENTY-THREE

Uma was the only guru at the head table when we walked into the dining room that evening. At her table sat Joseph, Brian, Abram, and the senator, along with three beautiful young women I hadn't remembered seeing before.

We found Danny and took our seats on either side of him. Katie was nowhere to be seen, so I assumed she really had gone home. *I sure wish I could talk to JJ to see what he may have learned.* Thankful that this was our last evening meal in silence, I wrote on my notepad and slid it in front of Danny. He nodded.

As soon as we were finished with our plated chicken dinner, both Danny and I excused ourselves to the restroom.

"Please be careful, Libby ..." he whispered as he handed me his phone. I walked into the ladies room which thankfully I found was empty.

Quickly, I dialed the Johnson household and JJ picked up on the third ring. Grateful they still had a home phone; it was the only number I could remember off the top of my head. I was also thankful that he hadn't ignored the unfamiliar number.

"Libby, I'm so glad you called," he said, once he heard my voice. "Listen, Katie is missing. Her parents are frantic. They said she called several days ago, frightened. She said she needed somewhere to stay and she'd be there the next day. She never showed."

"And, what did you learn about Jill?" I whispered.

"I haven't found anyone in her circle who knows anything. It doesn't appear she had many close friends, actually."

"JJ—I've witnessed enough ... well, let's just say several abnormal things. I think they drugged me last night. I'm having a difficult time remembering it all, but I do remember several things. I think they're hiding young girls..."

The bathroom door opened.

JJ prompted, "Go on, Libby ... I'm listening."

"Hello! Is that you, Bella?" I jovially asked the newcomer, praying that JJ would understand and not talk more. I wasn't sure what this person would be able to hear through the cell phone.

There was a pause, then a soft voice whispering, "No, not Bella ... but we're not supposed to talk."

"Sorry," I whispered back. "You're right. Hold on."

"What?"

I left it at that and prayed the woman would hurry and

be gone. JJ must have understood because the line was quiet as we waited for the lady to wash her hands and leave the room. I peeked through the space between the wall and stall door until I saw she was gone.

"Ok. Sorry. JJ, what did you learn about Love & Mercy?"

"I'm still waiting for some information to come back … so not much."

"I'm certain they are using this place as a front for something else. I can't say for sure what, but for a religious organization, a *lot* of money changes hands. Also, I keep seeing groups of young women—some are possibly not even of age—and they appear to be hiding them. There is an air of secrecy. Something doesn't smell right."

"Okay. I'll keep digging, but Libby … when do you come home?"

"Tomorrow is our last day here."

"I'm not sure what we'll learn in that time, but are you in danger?"

"Nah, I don't *think* so. Freaked out by a few people? Yes. But, I don't think they are on to me."

"Good. Keep it that way—don't go snooping around! Just finish the retreat and we'll see what we can learn about the missing girls."

"Yeah, yeah. Okay. Oh, did I tell you—or maybe Alexis knows? Brian is here at the retreat. So, at least Bella and I have a friend that could help us if needed."

"Brian from work?"

"Yeah. I had no idea either, until I got here."

"Be safe, Libby…"

"Oh! Also, can you call Greg and let him know I lost my phone? I really don't want him thinking I'm avoiding him or anything."

"Sure, will do!"

I carefully tucked the phone into the waistband of my skirt, opened the door, and walked right into Joseph.

"Hey, careful there, kiddo!" he laughed as he helped me get steady.

Danny quickly came over and took my arm. I wanted to ask Joseph why he stole my phone, but Danny whisked me off. I turned to look back at the slimy guy standing with one knee bent, his foot and back leaning against the wall. Once we were out of earshot, I turned to Danny.

"How long has he been standing there?"

"He had just walked up—don't worry."

I was still worried.

As we walked up to the dining room doors, diners were already making their way out. I tried looking over their heads for Bella, and decided to step aside and wait for her. Once everyone had filed out, I looked in again. The room was clear. She must have got by us so Danny and I followed the crowd to the chapel. Both of us edged around other patrons tossing back their juice shot. Again, we looked all over, but didn't find Bella. That's strange; I was sure she planned on attending tonight. Danny and I shrugged and picked seats anyway. Maybe she had changed her mind?

Tonight's lesson was centered around earth. All the elements we'd focused on during retreat came together tonight as being essential elements on earth. Uma—Kali wasn't on stage—led us through meditation, but all I could fixate on was wondering where Bella went. That led to fixating about Kali, too. Hadn't I witnessed the two gurus arguing earlier? Had Kali bowed out from sharing the stage with Uma because of that? My stomach was as unsettled as my brain. Where were people disappearing to? Was I being paranoid? I couldn't reconcile any of it, but felt I had to go with my gut feeling—something was brewing; nothing was as it seemed. Those were the consistent messages flowing through me.

When I heard the chime, I slowly opened my eyes. In my lap was a small envelope. I looked around the room, a few others were also now holding small envelopes. I glanced over at Danny; he had one. *Who put these in our laps?* How had I not felt someone there? I shivered, opening it up. 'You are chosen' was what the note inside said. Uma's voice, even though quiet, startled me.

"My lovelies, we have thoroughly enjoyed our time with you over the past several days. This was our final Satsang together, which means the end to the silence. Most of you have signed up for activities tomorrow so if that's you, we'll see you around and please enjoy the amenities. Otherwise, vans will be here promptly at nine tomorrow morning to transport you home." The volume in the room had increased, most people wanted to talk to those next to them now that the silence was lifted.

"Ladies and gentlemen, a few more things and then I promise you can talk the night away!" she waited until those talking had settled. "Thank you. Now, there are a handful of guests who received a small envelope. You are the lucky chosen ones! Please stay seated after your brothers and sisters have left. We hope to see everyone back for the next retreat. Namaste."

I wanted nothing more than to go back to the cabin and find Bella. I didn't know we had a choice to be on a van first thing in the morning. We *had* to get on that van—I saw no purpose in sticking around for more activities. I wanted to get to JJ and help him follow up his research. Danny nudged me.

"What do you suppose you're *chosen* for?" he asked.

I rolled my eyes, "I can't imagine, but really, all I want to do is leave this place!"

"I don't feel we've learned enough."

I looked at him questioningly.

"My daughter … Katie … Jill. Where are Katie and Jill? What happened to Bonnie?"

"Yes, I know. I feel that need too, but I have my detective friend looking into that from the outside. I'm really getting antsy to get out." I reached down to the floor, looking for my water bottle. Shoot, I had left it at the cabin. Before I pulled myself back up, I saw boots. I slowly moved back in my chair and looked up. Joseph was standing over me.

"Looking for something?"

"Yes. My phone!" I hissed.

Tsking, he said, "You know you can't have that here, Libby. How about a bottle of water instead?" He handed L&M monogrammed stainless-steel bottles to both Danny and me. He continued down the aisles to several rows behind us where a young lady sat. I watched him hand out water to the chosen ones as I chugged down the cold refreshment.

Uma sounded the gong. We all stopped talking and looked to the stage. "My lovelies … we will be taking a field trip for the final elemental activity of the trip."

Danny shouted out, "Why isn't everyone joining? Why only the 'chosen'?"

Her eyes softened and the syrupy sweet voice purred, "Ahhh, you shall see shortly. You all are privileged, I assure you. Please return to your residences and change into your comfy exercise clothing. Your butlers will pick you up in thirty minutes. Bring your water and we'll see you soon. Namaste." She bowed, then set her headset on the chair and slipped out the side of the stage.

Danny and I looked at each other skeptically, then got up to leave. When I turned to him, I noticed his eyes appeared glassy. "You okay?" He nodded, and I gave him a hug when he got to his place, "See you shortly," I smiled, mimicking Uma.

Our cabin wasn't far from Danny's, but the trail took several twists before I could see our front porch. The envelope I'd been carrying floated to the ground and I knelt down to pick it up. I stood, losing my balance, teetering side to side. *Whoa! Why so dizzy?* The sound of footfalls made me turn around, weaving again. Strong arms encircled me, clamping my arms behind my back. A leather clad hand muffled my screams, dragging me.

CHAPTER TWENTY-FOUR

Shhhhh…" the voice behind said. "Quiet and I'll remove my hand." He'd dragged me into the cabin.

I recognized this voice. I nodded in cooperation. As he released me, my eyes sought his—those deep brown eyes I couldn't seem to escape. Joseph was standing, ready to capture me again. I backed up a few steps, arms raised in defense. *Where was Shadow? Where's Bella?*

"What the hell?" I spat.

"Shhhhh. Libby, there are things I've got to tell you. And, I need your help."

My eyes wildly shifted around the room, looking for a way out. "Help? Why on earth would I help *you*? You've been terrorizing me the entire time I've been here! And, where is my phone?"

His smirk reminded me of why I was so frightened of him. I glanced to the cabin's door.

"Oh, no you don't." He reached out and grabbed my arm, leading me to the couch. "Libby, please, just sit down. I promise I won't touch you—I need you to listen."

It appeared I had no choice. He was stronger than me and he was blocking my way out of the cabin.

He reached into an inner jacket pocket and pulled out a black leather wallet-like object. When he flipped it open, I nearly lost my dinner.

"*What*? F-B-I ...?" My eyes fixated on the badge as my brain swirled trying to recall all the interactions we'd had. How had I not figured *that* out?

"Look. Libby, I'm on your side. I think you're on to something—I know you've been snooping around and have suspicions. Jill?"

"Yes! Jill! You two were dating ... wait a minute! You're not the CEO of some tech giant?" So many questions began to flood in. He was shaking his head no. He wasn't at all who everyone was saying.

"No, we never dated. She's working with us though. We gave the appearance we were an item for awhile, but no, we are not a couple. And, yes, I had to have a cover ... I've actually worked in the social media industry years back, uh, before this gig."

"Is she okay?"

"She is. But, she's gone deeper into the organization and mostly out of sight."

I felt a sigh of relief. "What exactly are you investigating? Where's my phone?"

"I told you before, I don't have your phone. What we're doing here—well, more specifics later. For tonight, I need your help; we're running out of time."

With eyes wide, I nodded. *I get to help the FBI?* This was getting interesting and my heartbeat sped up, waiting for the details.

"That water I handed you earlier…" he pointed to the stainless-steel container that he'd thrown on the couch after dragging me inside. "Yours wasn't tampered with; well, not much anyway, but they think it was. Everyone else was fully dosed."

"Dosed? You mean *drugged*?!"

"Yes, settle down. It's nothing that will permanently harm anyone. We've been micro-dosing you all since you arrived. But, tonight, the rest of 'em will be out for awhile. It's all part of this evening's 'earth activity'," he emphasized with the air quotes.

I swallowed hard. "Why me? Why are you trusting me to help?"

"I realized early on that you were here looking for Jill. I've been trying to thwart you and keep you away from messing with our investigation. Libby, you seriously don't know what you're getting yourself into. So, earlier this evening when I heard you on the phone with your police friend, I decided to bring you into the fold instead. Otherwise, you are getting close to blowing the whole operation."

Chills ran down my arms. *He had been listening to me in the bathroom. What had I said?*

"I don't understand how it is that I can help."

"Will you trust me?" He held up his badge again as though that was the key to trust.

"Do I have a choice?"

He shook his head. "Not really. Either help me, or I

have to get you out of the way."

Terrified of what that meant, I began again seeking a way to run.

"I don't mean *dead*; I'd send you home…" he clarified.

"Why would you do that? Just send me home. Why tell me any of this?"

"Well, you've seen too much already—and, as I already stated, I can't risk you blowing our operation."

"I knew *nothing* about your operation!"

He began to pace the floor. "Okay. Yes, I believe that now. But, you were getting close … pictures you took, snooping around, and witnessing everything that went down at that party. I either need your help, or I need to get you home."

"I barely remember that party. What happened there?"

"Libby, focus. We have to hurry! There'll be time to chat about it all later."

"Alright, alright. Jeez. What is it I need to do to help, specifically?"

"Can you act drugged and confused?"

"I suppose. I mean, what choice do I have? My friends are apparently involved in tonight's fun … I can't leave them here."

"Okay, then. That's what I need you to do. Go along with everything they're doing tonight and trust me."

"Where are Bella and Shadow?"

"Bella was walking her earlier, but I don't know where they are now."

"Promise me that you will help all of us—Bella, Danny, Shadow, and me. None of us are part of … whatever it is going on here. Please make sure we all get home safely."

"I promise." He held up three fingers in a good ol' Boy Scout promise.

CHAPTER TWENTY-FIVE

Badri pulled up outside.

"Ok, here we go … go limp, remember you are under the influence of powerful drugs. Don't break cover." I nodded from my place on the sofa where I was sprawled out. I felt weak; it might not be too difficult to act this one out.

"Badri is in on this?" I whispered.

He ignored me. "Shh!"

Never had I dreamed I'd be an actress. Of course, I'd also never imagined I'd be working with the FBI. As I lay there with my eyes closed, pretending to be dead to the world, I realized this must be a much bigger deal. *The FBI? Doesn't that mean federal crimes? The young girls—human trafficking? What had he said—they'd been micro-dosing us all along. Why?*

The front door opened and Joseph called Badri to come help him. They lifted my limp body and carried me to the golf cart.

I heard Badri ask innocently, "Why are Libby and Bella asleep? Where are we taking them?"

"You know better than to ask questions!" Joseph hissed. "Just do as the gurus ask!"

They climbed into the front seats after securing me on one of the back seat benches and Badri pulled away from the cabin, Joseph in the passenger seat. I discreetly opened one eye. I'd heard Bella's name mentioned, but couldn't see her. *And, where was my Shadow?*

I recognized the path we were on. My pulse quickened as I realized we were headed for the gravesites. *What have I gotten myself into?* Frantically, I wondered if I could jump from the vehicle and run for help instead. Help from whom? The place was highly guarded and frankly, I didn't know who I could trust. I never saw Joseph as being one of the good guys. Was I right in putting my trust in him? Should I have demanded to go home? Probably. But, what would that have meant for Bella and Danny? They were already drugged and who knew what was going to happen. No, it was good for me to stay aware and work with him instead of against him. I hoped so anyway.

My ribs were aching from getting tossed about on the bumpy dirt road. I wanted to shift position but didn't dare move. Would they even notice, though? I tried slightly shifting as we hit a large pothole. *Son of a … ouch!*

After what felt like an eternity, we stopped. I could feel warmth and I smelled the smoke of a campfire.

From one of the bench seats behind me, I heard Bella

stir. "Where are we?" she slurred. I remained still.

Joseph and Badri walked to the back of the cart and I could tell they were helping Bella up. It sounded as though she was conscious. When I peeked, I saw they were walking her toward a fire pit. They sat her in a chair next to a couple of others. Joseph came back to the cart on his own.

Bending down over me, he whispered directly in my ear. "Mimic how others are behaving, okay? They're coming to, but are very groggy. Do the same." I nodded as he lifted me up. I allowed him to assist me walking over to the campfire and I clumsily slumped into the chair provided. I didn't make eye contact with anyone, but kept my eyes partially open, acting drowsy.

I could make out silhouettes of several people standing behind the glow of the campfire. No detail, just black outlines. Sensing people on either side of me, I slowly rolled my head and caught a glimpse of Bella and then to the other side, Danny. I couldn't tell if anyone else had joined us.

"How much did you give these guys?" a man's voice asked someone standing close to me. I kept my eyes closed.

"Enough. Don't worry." The responding man's voice was familiar. The next thing I knew, he kicked my shin. *Ouch!* "See, no reaction."

"Yes, but she said the whole idea is to have them alert enough to know what's going on. They have to willingly *want* to be buried—to experience facing their worst fears."

My pulse shot up. *What? Buried?* I had figured we were headed in the direction of the gravesites, but I couldn't imagine they were actually going to … *I could trust Joseph, right?*

The familiar voice I hadn't placed yet said, "Give them

enough time. We still have to wait for Uma to arrive and do all her hocus pocus—by then, they'll be more alert, right?"

With that, I heard logs being thrown onto the fire. Flames grew large, five feet high, licking the cool night air. Silence fell all around. I felt Bella move in her chair next to me; she groaned, "Mmm, warm…"

Danny's head turned and now we were staring at each other. The fear in his eyes was palpable, but it appeared the rest of his body was paralyzed. I tried to communicate through my eyes to let him know we'd be okay. *But, would we? Where had Joseph gone?* I hadn't heard his voice since he'd helped me into my chair.

Bella moved again and I flipped my head back her direction. "Mom…" I heard her say. I looked again toward the fire, but with the bright glow, I still couldn't make out who was standing there. I looked back over to Bella and her eyes were closed again. She must have been dreaming.

What was the purpose to all this? I was getting impatient and wanted Joseph to do something. *Where was he? Where were the SWAT teams? Isn't that how it happened in the movies?*

The heat from the fire had diminished. I wondered how long we'd been sitting here. And, what exactly *were* we waiting for. Then, I felt it—flowing silk fabric tickled my face. I turned. She had arrived … Uma was standing over me, smiling a devilish grin. Softly, she brushed her fingernails over my shoulders, my face, then up through my scalp. It sent chills throughout my body and took every ounce of my will to stay still. Moving between each of us, she continued this while speaking in tongues. At least, I could not understand what she was chanting. I grew impatient once again—*what was with this satanic-like ritual? What was she doing?*

"Hello again, my lovelies," she cooed. "I'm so happy you chose to join us tonight."

Chose?

"Yes, you are the chosen ones. Our sacrifices are what bring us enlightenment and you've made an important choice tonight." She taunted before chanting once again.

Being lulled by Uma's voice, I tried to break the hypnosis by tuning her out. I wondered where Kali was. Was she also part of all this? She seemed so practical, down to earth. I couldn't imagine her condoning what Uma was planning here.

I turned back to look at Danny. He moved his fingers this time; maybe the drugs were wearing off. I softened my gaze with him, trying to signal it would be alright. I kept trying to convince myself that it would.

A man's voice broke into the silence that followed Uma's chanting.

"We're not actually going to bury them, are we?" He moved from behind the flames and now I could see it was Abram who had asked the question. I listened intently to their conversation. "You said earlier this activity was about finding enlightenment."

"Exactly! They *will* find enlightenment—in the earth!" She laughed wickedly, her flaming red hair spiking out in every direction. "Now, stop questioning me. You ... and, uh, you ... help move this one over to that hole there."

"Uh, Uma ... hold on now. Where's Kali? We can't possibly actually bury human beings. Surely, this enlightenment activity was meant to be carried out differently."

Her cackling laughter let us all know how false his belief was.

I heard feet moving and men grunting. Tilting my head toward the noise, I opened my eyes a bit wider. I could see one hole had already been filled in with dirt. Was that a PVC pipe protruding? It was hard to see. Slowly inching my head around again, I saw they were moving Danny. Two men helped his weakened body to walk. Danny's eyes were open and he tried looking back at me. He had no control though, his head slumped forward.

The FBI was going to allow my friend to be buried alive? Certainly not! Where was Joseph? I needed to do something! Terror grabbed me when one of the men who had Danny turned toward me. Those familiar green eyes bore right into mine. *Brian?*

CHAPTER TWENTY-SIX

My arms and legs felt heavy, sluggish. My brain screamed to run and get away. They put Danny into the hole and were shoveling dirt over him; I felt paralyzed—with fear, or actually incapacitated—I couldn't be sure. Panic washed over me as I saw a man with a ballcap approach. Abram! He was the one I'd seen several times before wearing a cap. Eyes wide open, I watched Brian and Abram pick up Bella.

"I can carry this one," Abram said.

"No, it's important that she walk. She's chosen this path."

Brian looked back at me. My eyes implored—how was this happening? Brian was our *friend*. I shuddered as his red hair and green eyes reflected the fire. He looked like something straight out of those horror films I hated so much. Memories flooded; my brain trying to make sense of a trusted friend turned torturous demon. All the many lunches, dinners, hikes … I'd confided in him! Had there been clues all along that I ignored? How could someone I trusted and invited into my own home now be involved in … in what? A cult?

Uma's chanting infiltrated my consciousness again. *Why couldn't I understand what she was saying? Was it really the Sanskrit prose I'd become used to during meditation?* No, not even close. It was nonsensical; I'd never heard people talking in tongues, but I'd imagine it'd sound similar. I turned to get her within my view again. She was dancing around the fire, spreading her wings, twirling around and chanting. Louder and louder. Sparks flying high above her, she twirled faster, the breeze she created spreading sparks farther into the dark sky. Was I dreaming? Was this really happening?

The hands prying me from the chair startled me. Kicking, punching, screaming out—I was not going to let them take me from my chair.

"Joseph!" came out of me as a blood curdling scream. "Help! Help us!"

I heard a bark.

Hot breath pierced my right ear. "There's no one to save you, Libby." Abram's menacing voice had an unmistakable bite.

I drove an elbow right into his ribs; kicked my heel into his groin. Shadow leapt from the darkness and knocked him down to the ground. Abram was momentarily stunned as I squirmed to my feet.

"C'mon, Shadow!" I yelled out, running down the path. Abram gave chase but I was much faster than the

guru's boyfriend. Veering off and into the thick brush—
the darkness enveloped everything once I was away from
the fire. *Where was Joseph? Had he lied to me? Led me like a lamb
to its slaughter?*

Once I was certain I'd lost Abram, I began to loop
around to get to the guru palace. Certainly, they had a
phone. I looked all over for Shadow; I had no idea where
she'd gone and I prayed she was okay. My lungs burned,
my legs felt like noodles, but I pressed forward, running
for my life. And Bella's. And Danny's. *Where was the FBI,
dammit!* Tears flowed down my face as I remembered my
friends being hauled away. *Were they already buried? Dead
under the compression of the dirt?* In the distance, I saw soft
lights. I prayed it was the residence. I felt lost and helpless;
floundering in the dark to find my way and worried my dog
was lost.

As I neared, I slowed and observed the surroundings.
It was quiet. Not a soul to be seen. The large building cast
ominous shadows, tricking my senses into seeing dark
monsters all around. I squatted down behind the trunk of
an enormous tree to catch my breath. I kept my eyes locked
on the windows where light shone—were there people in
there? I couldn't be sure they weren't in on this.

How do I know who is good and who is bad? Right now, I had
to take my chances … my friends' lives depended on it. I
rose and slunk around the tree, stealthily making my way
closer to the building. Maybe I could at least find a weapon
in there. It was worth the risk. Find something to use as a
weapon and find a phone. Satisfied that I had a plan, I kept
going.

Crouching low along a wall, I listened and quietly
proceeded toward the glass doors ahead. I took the steps,

two at a time, then reached out for the door handle. An enormous figure appeared as I twisted the doorknob.

CHAPTER TWENTY-SEVEN

Of course, there was security at the guru palace. The same hulk of a security guard who took our electronics on the first day stood in front of me.

"Can I help you?" his deep gravelly voice questioned.

Frozen in place, my dilated eyes stared back. Mouth gaping open, I couldn't speak. *Who were my enemies here? Could I trust this guard?*

"Uh, could … could I please, uh," I swallowed hard, "borrow the telephone, please?" My body shook from his menacing glare.

After what seemed hours, he stepped aside, "Sure, miss. This way."

My feet wouldn't budge, they felt nailed down.

"C'mon, now. You look cold. Come inside—phone's

this way." His large hands reached out and touched my shoulder. I jumped, turning sideways, creeping by him through the doorway. He passed me and led the way down the hall.

I looked into each room as we went by. No one.

"Uh, where is everyone?" I asked.

"Big activities tonight, I hear … suppose that's where everyone's at." He stopped and I nearly ran into the back of him. I took a couple steps back. "What are you so scared of anyway?" he asked.

He seemed helpful now, maybe I could trust him with the information. I needed help immediately … what choice did I have but to enlist his? "My friends are in trouble. I really need to call for help."

"Well, why didn't you say something sooner?" he reached for his shoulder microphone. "Unit two, we need assistance at the main residence. Unit two, copy?"

Once he was sure help was on the way, he signaled for me to continue following him. My nerves began to settle.

"Is Kali here?" I cautiously asked.

"Nope, she was with everyone else—last I knew anyway. Here, let's get some tea. Right this way." He led me into a sitting room, similar to the one I'd visited in before, but I noticed this one had no windows and was considerably smaller. "Go ahead, take a seat."

He left the room and promptly came back with a tea set. As much as I loved tea parties, my friends were in danger and I found myself getting impatient.

"Thank you for your kindness." I looked up at him after pretending to take a sip. "But, I really need to get back to my friends; I'm worried about them. Can I please use a phone? We don't have much time."

He looked curious, and laughed. "What kind of danger could they possibly be in, here at the resort?"

Despair set in. No one was going to believe that a guru was burying my friends alive. I recognized that this was the craziest sounding accusation. Who would believe me?

"The FBI has an undercover agent here. Two agents actually." I heard myself spewing the words, realizing they weren't making this story sound any less crazy. "Joseph. You know, Joseph Banter! I saw you guys talking a few days ago. He confided in me earlier … said there's a big operation going down tonight. He wanted my help. So, I agreed and was playing along. My friends are being buried right now. He disappeared. Something has happened to him!"

"Hold on, hold on. Being buried?" he scoffed. "C'mon now!"

I nodded my head as tears started to flow.

"I know it sounds super crazy. But, I'm serious. Uma! She's chanting wacked-out devilish stuff…" I saw the look on his face. He most definitely judged that I was the only one who was bat-shit crazy here.

"Uma? The guru?" He shook his head. "That's not possible. I saw her before you showed up."

My eyes grew wide. *Was she here in the house? She left the bonfire?* My head whipped around, looking for the exits. *I am not crazy.* I need to get out of here and find Joseph.

"Lady, just settle down. I'll go meet up with my security officers outside. You keep sipping your tea. I'll be right back." He backed out of the doorway, keeping his eyes on me until he pulled the door closed.

I jumped up, headed to the door. Then I heard it—the click. I yanked hard at the doorknob—it didn't budge. I'd been locked in the room.

"HELP!" I kept screaming, hoping one of the staff would hear me. Where was everyone?

CHAPTER TWENTY-EIGHT

The campfire embers barely glowed, but otherwise the desert was pitch black. No sign of anyone left behind after the earlier celebration. Everything looked calm. The two security guards got back into their golf cart and slowly moved along the path.

"I think the hysterical woman Mike spoke of is on something." The man driving said to the other, using his finger in a loop beside his head, indicating crazy.

"Yep, sounds like she sure thought her friends were in danger. But, I think everyone's hit it for the night. Let Mike know there's nothing to see here."

"Did he ask Uma about this?"

"Not yet; said her quarters were already dark when he went by. I agree with him—don't poke the bear, you know?"

"Yep, agreed. She's a monster when disturbed."

"What about Kali?"

"I haven't seen her since earlier this morning. Probably an offsite function to attend—busy lady."

"We should drive through the camp to check things out. Don't want to be accused of not thoroughly doing our job."

* * *

Exhausted from trying to beat the door down, I slumped to the floor. I listened carefully for any sign of life. It was eerily silent. Sitting with knees bent, I folded my arms and rested my head as I tried to come up with my next move.

I was stunned that Brian was involved. What did I actually see? Well, he dragged my friends off and tried to get me. Where had he taken them, though? I presumed from how the men had talked, Danny and Bella were going into those holes. *Had I actually seen that though?* I was so confused—who knew what was real anymore? It was so dark out there. If it was a celebration or activity as they were calling it, then why weren't more of the resort guests attending? *Why were we the chosen for enlightenment?* I couldn't wrap my head around any of it. Had I lost my mind? What I'd seen—was it criminal? If the FBI were involved in bringing the organization down for whatever reason, then where were they right now?

I heard something. I jumped to my feet and began looking for something that could be used as a weapon. Scanning the room, my eyes landed on the fireplace. I ran over and grabbed the poker from its holder. Back at the door, I pressed my ear against it and listened. There were several voices—soft spoken, didn't sound as though they had a sense of urgency. *Are they good guys? Or bad guys?* That was the big question as I contemplated revealing, or hiding, myself. The footfalls sounded as though they passed by my door and were moving away.

"HELP!!" I screamed, praying that it wasn't one of the maniacs.

Banging as hard as I could, I listened for a second before I started shouting again.

In the space at the bottom of the door, I saw a shadow. "Someone be there?" a small feminine voice asked in broken English. The doorknob jiggled.

"Yes! Please, help. It's locked."

Two girls began talking between themselves in a language I didn't recognize. The doorknob moved again, this time a little more frantically.

"Do you have keys?" I shouted.

The chatter of the girls started to fade away. They were walking away.

"No! Don't leave!"

Complete silence filled the air again. I stretched out on the floor, trying to see anything under the door. No one was standing there. Tears ran down my face. I was so sure they were staff members who would have keys—*why wouldn't they open the door?*

Feeling defeated, my limbs completely exhausted, I curled up on the floor waiting for any other sign of life. I needed a plan—what would I do when I got released? Defend myself … find my friends and Shadow; call for police. Top priority was to get away and find people that would help me. Clearly the security guards were not helping!

Someone approached the door; the knob moved as I heard the familiar metallic sound of a key being inserted. I jumped behind the door, bracing myself with the poker held high above my head. The door slowly opened and I charged forward, swinging.

CHAPTER TWENTY-NINE

"Whoa! Lady!" the behemoth security guard had reached out, skillfully grabbing the poker right from my hand. "I told you I'd be right back."

I punched at him, fighting to get around his large form and out the door. He threw the poker across the room, snatched my arms and pulled them behind me in one swift move.

Kicking and yelling, I shouted, "Why did you lock me in here?"

"For your protection. Would you hold still? I don't want to hurt you."

"Let me go!" I thrashed, trying to get free.

"If you'll stop, I will!" he growled, slowly releasing my hands. "Now, *calm down* so I can update you on what my guys found."

He had my attention. I held a defensive stance and was ready to leap for the poker again, if necessary.

"Listen, we drove over to where the bonfire was tonight. No one was there. The fire had died to embers."

Tears were streaming down my face. He didn't believe me. Breathless, I choked out, "My friends are there! They buried them!"

"We didn't find any evidence of that, ma'am."

"Take me there. *Please…*" I pleaded with eyes full of tears.

"Okay. C'mon. Follow me."

I wanted to grab the fireplace tool. He saw my glance that direction and gave me the eye. I followed obediently

"Do you have a flashlight and shovel?"

He rolled his eyes, but led me to an outside shed where he grabbed a shovel. His hand tapped the flashlight on his belt. We loaded into the golf cart and sped off into the night. I kept my eye open for Shadow—*where had she gone?*

"You didn't see a black dog roaming around when you were out here earlier, did you?"

"Nah. No dog."

My heart hurt. *What have I done? How had Shadow managed to find us at that fire pit anyway?* Last I'd heard from Joseph, Bella was walking her. They must have nabbed Bella, Shadow ran free … my stomach lurched. There was no good scenario. Bella was clearly drugged when I last saw her. *Did she even know what was happening to her?*

After ten minutes or so, we pulled up to the still-smoldering fire.

"Flashlight?" I held my hand out demanding. He handed it over. "Leave the cart's lights on—shining there."

I pointed to a mound of dirt twenty feet away, hopped out of the vehicle, grabbed the shovel, and beelined it to where I'd seen holes earlier.

I looked around confused. Earlier, I'd seen one that was filled in—a PVC pipe sticking out of it. My head whipped around, looking for that one. Each hole was sitting empty, exactly as I'd seen them in the daylight.

The security guard came up behind me. "Ah, I see now … there are holes. Couldn't see them from the road."

"This one—it was filled in earlier. Someone was buried there." I turned around and pointed. "Over there, that's where they dragged my friend Danny." We both walked carefully around the open holes and stood over the one I was sure we'd find Danny in.

"Are you sure you didn't have too much juice today?" he laughed. Anger flashed from my eyes. He hung his head. "Sorry. Of course not."

I demonstrated exactly where everyone was earlier, miming who did what, when, and where. His eyes followed each of my movements. When I was done, he shook his head in disbelief.

"I want to believe you. I really do. But, where are they *now*?"

"I don't know! That's what I need help with!" I screamed, feeling completely helpless. "Can you drive me to my cabin?"

He nodded yes and off we went.

As we pulled up, I checked my watch. As much as time seemed to fly by, it also felt as though it had stood still. It was near one o'clock in the morning. Wasn't it after nine when Satsang was over? Nearly ten I assumed by the time we got to the bonfire. *Hours had passed since I had run off.*

They could be anywhere.

As soon as the cart stopped, I hopped out and ran up the steps. I flung open the door, praying to see Shadow in her bed and Bella in her room. Flipping on lights, everything was exactly as we left it; no one occupied the cabin.

I ran out the door, down the steps, and sprinted down the lane toward Danny's. The behemoth was surprisingly light on his feet and kept up. Bolting through Danny's door, hoping I'd wake him if he were there, I reached for the light switch. Vacant.

My head was spinning. What the hell was going on? Where was everyone? I bent over with my hands on my knees, hyperventilating.

I turned my head to the guard. "Where are they?" I stood straight, walking around the kitchen counter.

He looked confused.

"YOU know everything that goes on at this place! WHERE ARE THEY?!" I screamed, with my finger right in his face.

"Ma'am, I have no idea. I would have thought everyone would be asleep at this hour."

"Wait, you said Uma was back at her residence. I want to talk to her. NOW!" I was shaking. "Now! Kali or Uma—I demand answers and I want to see them right now."

Surprisingly, there was no objection.

"C'mon. We'll go wake them." He turned to leave; I grabbed Danny's phone that was left on his countertop and stashed it in my pocket.

We walked back outside and hopped into the cart. After the second turn he took, I realized we weren't headed toward the guru's residence.

"Where are we going?" I asked alarmed.

Silence.

CHAPTER THIRTY

"WHERE ARE WE GOING?" I screamed, and punched his arm.

"You'll see."

On the next turn, I knew exactly where we were headed. The Employees Only sign was to our left and shortly after, I saw the familiar maintenance buildings.

"You said Uma was in the residence."

"No, I said I'd seen her before you arrived … I never said where."

He wasn't wrong. I may have inferred she was at her residence.

We drove up to the front of the main building. Once he shut the golf cart off, we were enveloped in blackness.

"Flashlight?" he said.

I felt around, but realized I think it got left back at the cabin. "I don't have it."

He sighed loudly, then got out of the vehicle. I followed. "What is this?" He didn't answer. I struggled to see as we ascended steps.

He knocked on the door. There was no movement or sound from inside. He knocked again.

"Door shouldn't be locked—just open it." I reached out to do so, and found it locked. "Okay, so much for *we don't lock doors here*—clearly, you do!" Irritated, I began to pace along the front porch.

He knocked again a little louder, then started peering in windows along the north side of the building. I heard movement. It hadn't come from inside the house. I looked down below my feet through the wooden slats that made up the decking. *What was that?*

Cautiously, I went down the steps and walked along the patio to the far south end. There was a cellar door! Something thumped from the inside—I was sure of it! Reaching down for the metal handle, I was slammed into the ground. I couldn't see anything, but felt the weight and the body heat as I was pinned to the earth. "Get off me, you lunk!" *Why was the guard tackling me now?* He had plenty of opportunity earlier.

I struggled, kicking and yelling. Then, I got a clear view the of the man straddling me. "Brian! Get off of me! What are you doing?"

He didn't say anything. A fist slammed the side of my head and everything went black.

CHAPTER THIRTY-ONE

The voices were distant, but clear.

"Did you call Uma?"

"Not yet. She's going to be furious. Nothing has gone according to plan."

"Yeah, because *you* didn't properly drug that snoopy dog lady!" he condemned.

Whose voices? I struggled as I tried opening my eyes. Pain shot through my skull and I tried grasping my head in my hands. My wrists were bound in zip ties. *Ugh!* I shut my eyes again, willing the pain to disappear and trying to remember what I'd seen in that brief moment. I lay still, feeling my hip bones drilling into the hard cold concrete. Carefully, I gradually opened them again. I tilted my head, enduring the pain of opening my eyes. Candlelight barely lit the room. Someone was in a chair slumped over. *Asleep? Dead? Who is that?* I blinked a few more times, trying to focus. It was the security guard. *Great.*

"What do we do now?"

"Well, we've got to get rid of them, first off. They were all supposed to be gone before sunrise."

I gulped. *Who? Danny, Bella, and me?*

"Yes, I know. We only have a few more hours before daylight. We need to figure this out. And, before *that* one comes to."

Footfalls sounded. They were close. My heart sped up and I willed my body to stay still. I could feel the heat from whoever knelt down near me. Face to face, I could feel his breath.

"She's out cold."

"Ok, good. Now, go get the vans ready. We'll have a guard drive one, I'll drive the other."

"You knocked out Mike—who else is there?"

"The night shift at the shack."

"They won't talk, will they?"

"Nah."

I could hear them step away. My mind raced—vans, where were they taking us? None of this made sense. Where was the FBI? Had Joseph tricked me into going with him using a fake badge or something?

A door opened and squeaked shut again. I felt cool air brush past. I'm near a door, I thought—good to know, might come in handy. When I trusted that both men were out of the room, I tried moving my feet. They were not bound—also good to know. Movement nearby paralyzed me again. I snuck a peek through my eye lashes and saw that the guard was stirring.

Assuming, since he was knocked out, that he was one of the good guys. I whispered, hoping he'd hear me, "Shh, lay still." He didn't move anymore, whether he heard me or not.

Another breeze swept over me and I heard the squeak of the door. My eyes snapped shut.

"Joe! The van is backed up to the porch. Let's go!"

A flurry of footsteps sounded. I remained comatose-still with my brain activity seemingly screaming for me to run. I couldn't move.

For what felt like an hour, I could hear multiple people shuffle by me. Terrified, I wanted to see what was happening but was too afraid to even peek. I braced myself for when I'd be the next one picked up and thrown into the back of the van.

"Hurry! Get 'em out!" one man hissed.

"I'm going as fast as I can. They're dead weight! It's not that easy."

I ventured a look and could see the guard still slumped in his chair. How many people were in this place? I hadn't counted how many times they'd passed by me, but there were more people here than only Bella, Danny, the guard, and me.

"Ok, van is full. They'll go in the next one. Be back soon!"

The door slammed.

I waited for sounds of the van driving off, then opened my eyes. Joseph was standing over me with a knife.

CHAPTER THIRTY-TWO

I cringed as he came down over me with the knife. "Don't kill me. I haven't seen anything. I know nothing." My eyes squeezed tight, but my body was unable to move.

"Stop it, Libby! I need to…" I moved and he yelled. "Stay still!" He quickly sliced the zip ties and then moved over to the guard. "We have to hurry. He'll be back."

I sat up. Lightning pain shot through my head and my stomach turned. I panted, leaning over, holding my head.

Joseph was shaking the guard. "Mike, c'mon … get up!" He cut off his zip ties also. "C'mon, man."

Mike moaned and stirred. His eyes caught mine first as they opened. He grimaced and reached for his skull. He must have expected to find it bleeding as he examined his hands.

"Guys, we've gotta get Bella and Danny. Shadow is here too."

I stood suddenly, holding onto the back of the sofa. "They're all here? Where?"

He pointed down. "There's a cellar. Let's go!"

The guard stood cautiously. We both followed Joseph down a hallway. Most of the bedroom doors were open and I looked in as we passed. No one was left in the main house. Joseph opened a door into a dark cavern below. He flipped a switch and it provided a faint glow as we carefully descended the stairs. I first locked eyes on Shadow whining in the corner, tied to a post. I ran to her.

"Oh, baby girl … I'm so sorry!" She squirmed, licked, and whined as I struggled to untie her. "Joseph, where's your knife?" He brought it over, and we cut the rope. She jumped into my arms, squealing and rubbing against me. I felt her all over for injuries and couldn't find any. *Thank God!*

Next, I turned to my friends. Mike and Joseph got the zip ties off of Bella and Danny. They were groggy, but coming to. I went to Bella and hugged her.

"Are you okay?" I checked her over for injuries. She looked unharmed. Her eyes were glassy and confused. "You'll be okay. We're here now and you're going to be fine." I continued scanning the large basement area, wondering why they were here—what was this all about? Then, I saw a dark lump in the far corner. I cautiously got up and walked across the room.

"Guys, over here!" They ran over and lifted the blanket; underneath was Katie. That got Danny's attention and he stumbled over. After cutting her restraints, we checked for a pulse. She had one, but it was faint—she must have been drugged too. We shook her around a bit, trying to wake her.

I panicked. "We have to get out of there! They'll be back…"

Danny's eyes grew large. "Libby, *he's* the one who drugged us and brought us here!" he pointed directly at Joseph, while also reaching for the knife in my hands. I backed away, out of his reach.

"No! Danny … he's good."

"You told me he was creepy!"

"Well, he was. But that was before I knew he was with the FBI."

His eyes settled on Joseph, skeptical that he was to be trusted. "FBI?" he questioned as Joseph reached in his jacket and produced his credentials. At the same time, the guard, Mike, brandished his badge as well. My jaw dropped.

"You've been working with him all along?" I pointed between the two men.

Mike nodded his head impatiently. "Look, guys. We can explain everything later. Right now, we need to get all of you out of here before that scary Irish dude returns!"

Joseph agreed, adding, "It won't be long before Uma gets wind of this too … we need to go!" He picked up the still unconscious Katie and started up the stairway.

I helped Bella off the floor and she leaned against me until she got her balance. Slowly, we worked our way up out of the cellar, through the main house, and onto the front patio. Not far off the patio was another van. Joseph got Katie lying down across the first set of back row seats. The rest of us piled in behind to the third-row seats. Mike buckled himself into the passenger seat and Joseph fired up the van. He peeled out of the driveway and turned right.

"Wait! The entrance is that way!" I shouted, pointing left.

"I know."

"We have to help Katie! What are you doing?"

"You'll see…"

CHAPTER THIRTY-THREE

After having convinced Danny they were the good guys, I heard him whisper close to me, "See?"

I nudged him and gave him a look. "Shh."

We pulled up in front of the guru's residence. "Why are we here?" I questioned.

Danny and Bella both asked, "Where are we exactly?" as their gaping mouths and large eyes admired the lighted building with an entrance as grand as any royal palace.

Joseph told us to stay put. "We have business to take care. Ready?" he asked Mike. They both exited the vehicle, leaving us sitting there.

I crawled forward over the seats to check on Katie. As I felt for a pulse, she started to move slightly. Her pulse felt stronger than before, I thought.

"Libby, I tell you … those two are up to no good!" Danny warned.

"They are FBI!"

"I'm not so sure about that."

Bella asked quietly, "Is this where you came for that party?"

"No, that's yet another part of this compound."

She nodded. "What do they want with us? Why tie us in that cellar?" Shadow whined.

I didn't know how to answer. "What did they tell you … when they took you there?"

"I don't remember anything at all."

Danny kept staring out the window. "I don't like this. We're sitting ducks here, you know."

"What do you want to do?"

"Run…"

Before he got the words out, we saw movement. The two agents each had a person in handcuffs and they were leading them to the van.

"See … agents. I told you." I smiled.

They opened the sliding door and struggled to get Uma and Senator Maizer seated in the middle row, right in front of ours. After shoving them in place, restraining their hands and feet, and slamming the door closed again, the guard and Joseph climbed back in and we were off.

"I *knew* you'd be a problem!" Uma spat the words back at me. I kicked her seat and watched her thrust forward. "We should have never invited you—you nosy thing!"

The Senator sat quietly. Then out of nowhere, "You know I have people. You'll regret this!"

I stared at the back of both of their heads, wanting to fly over the seat and pummel them. They'd scared the crap out of all of us. I couldn't stay quiet any longer. Quietly, I pulled out Danny's phone that I'd grabbed earlier.

"Who the hell buries people for the fun of it? For a retreat activity?" I yelled at Uma.

"Oh, stop being so melodramatic, Libby. They could breathe!"

Ah, so they had actually done it. I hadn't been absolutely sure till now. "Out of a PVC pipe you expected them to breathe?"

Uma scoffed. I noticed the senator turn to stare at Uma. *Had he known of this?* It didn't appear so.

"Who were all the young folks we hauled out tonight?" I yelled to Joseph.

The guru quickly spoke up. "They're my staff!" she said indignantly.

Joseph's eyes met mine in the rear-view mirror. "Or, illegal immigrants those two were trafficking."

My mouth gaped.

The senator protested. "You can't prove that! I don't know what you're talking about!"

"Well, maybe you weren't fully aware of where all your donations came from—or *how*, rather—but you were certainly involved in this operation. We've followed the money. You and several other government officials."

"That's ridiculous! All the money we've generated have been from religious courses—self-help courses! You don't know anything!" Uma screamed. She was becoming more and more agitated as the drive went on.

Danny piped up after sitting quietly, listening to it all. "So, your *members* are funding your trafficking operation. That's why it's impossible to make it through all the levels—you make it impossible in order to continually launder more money," he stated. "*Members* felt they had no way out once they were buried in debt. And, how exactly did you make them work off their debt, huh? Emily felt there was no way out—*why*?" His face was beet red now and he leaned over the seat, got right up in Uma's face, "You killed my daughter!"

Mike turned in his seat. "Hey man, let's bring the temperature down. I know you're angry. These two will be going away for a very long time. Don't worry."

At first, I wasn't sure that Danny would let it go. After an uncomfortable minute, he slowly sat back. "They better pay. My daughter deserved better and I'm never going to forget what *this* woman put her through!"

I patted his hand. "They're caught now."

We sat in silence for a few minutes. Some of the dots had connected for me, but I still didn't understand how this large organization had been around for so many years. Had this illegal trafficking gone on all along? Was that why it was established in the first place?

Uma whipped her head around and glared at me. The Senator had become awfully quiet, saying nothing, and keeping his eyes down. We passed through the front gates of the property and continued down the highway toward Patagonia. Even though the belongings we'd brought were still in our respective cabins, it didn't appear to matter to any of us. I could feel the collective sigh of relief after we'd escaped the compound grounds. Even Katie had woken, sitting up to look around.

When she turned to the back seat behind her, she panicked. "No … no…!" She was looking directly at Senator Maizer.

CHAPTER THIRTY-FOUR

We pulled up at a sheriff's substation in Patagonia. Red and blue lights lit up the entire pre-dawn sky. A helicopter flew above, shining its spotlight down on the area. The residents, I'm sure, didn't appreciate this type of early awakening. I, for one, was appreciative of the police presence. Besides the Sheriff's Department, I saw DPS, FBI, ambulances, and unmarked police cars everywhere. I'd never felt more comforted.

Officers surrounded our van, opening the sliding doors. Shadow barked and I grabbed tighter to her harness, even though we were squeezed way in the back. One woman helped Katie out and led her over to an ambulance. Two other officers grabbed Uma and the senator and led them, barely shuffling with their feet tied, to one of the sheriff's

SUVs. Joseph and Mike helped us out of the back row of the van.

Danny shook Joseph's hand. "I'm sorry, man. I had it wrong. Thank you for getting us out alive."

"No problem." He looked to the rest of us. "We'll need you all to give your statements this morning. Our SUV is right over there. Unless you need medical attention first?"

We all felt much better and didn't feel the need for the medics.

"Will we wait for Katie?" I asked, looking toward the ambulance.

"We can stop by and see if they're going to release her. If so, then yes," Joseph answered; we all began walking to her. We were offered coffee and we sipped the warm drink while waiting for Katie to receive some IV fluids. Once her vitals were acceptable to the medics, they cleared her to leave.

* * *

On the four-hour drive back to the city, we had a lot questions.

"Uma indicated she had buried you guys…" I stated, looking between Bella and Danny. "Is that true?"

They shrugged and looked to the front seat. Joseph nodded.

"Yep. Unfortunately."

Irritated, I spat, "Why would you let that happen!?"

"It's complicated, Libby. We needed more evidence to have an iron-clad case, or that nut job would get away again."

"Uma? *Again*?"

"She's been on our radar for years. But, she's slick.

Everything she does is under an umbrella of religion. Do you know how difficult it is to bring down a religious organization?"

"That's no religion—Love & Mercy," I scoffed.

Mike spoke up. "Actually, it is. Kali has built a reputable place …"

I cut him off. "Kali! Where is she? Will she be arrested too?"

"No, that's what I'm trying to tell you guys. She actually helped us catch Uma. This latest retreat was specifically planned to trap those involved with illegal activities."

"So she figured it out and came to you …"

"Something like that. Like I said, we've been investigating human and drug trafficking in the area for years. A couple years back, we were able to trace the money to Love & Mercy. We questioned Kali; she was clueless about what was going on behind her back. Thankfully, she was extremely helpful—she really wanted to save her spiritual sanctuary and protect the members."

Danny had been soaking up all the information, but couldn't remain silent any longer. "They killed my Emily. I want them to pay."

"We know about your past police reports related to Emily. Our condolences." Mike lowered his head. "Five years ago, right?"

Danny nodded.

"Yes, that's when we got involved. The police filled us in on your suspicions."

Danny's head perked up. "I didn't think they'd listened to me at all. That's why I joined the church—to start my own investigation." He smiled.

"Yep, we've been watching you, too. That's why when

you befriended Libby … we, well Joseph, started following you all."

"I knew you were on to something, and it turns out you were instrumental in helping me," Joseph said.

"How so?"

"Well, first off … I wasn't entirely sure where they'd placed Jill. But when I followed you on one of your many walks, I discovered that maintenance area. I was able to connect with Jill."

I thought back to all the times I was certain he was following me. He was.

"And, my man JJ said you wouldn't leave well enough alone." I looked up to the mirror where Joseph was looking directly at me.

"You know Jeff Johnson?"

He nodded. "We worked together years back. He called me this week, asking about Jill Walsh—he knew she was an informant assisting us and I guess you were asking about her."

Wow, I had no idea.

"Also, you were instrumental because Uma discovered your snooping and that's how she came up with 'the chosen' earth activity. That was never on the plan prior. She wanted you and your friends out of the way. Once she knew that you knew where the girls were being stashed, she wanted you dead."

My pulse quickened.

Bella was still fixated on Joseph's revelations. "Jill works for the FBI?"

"Yep, she's been assisting us. She came forward several weeks ago—concerned for several friends of hers. We had to make it look like she quit and went back to California.

But, you two wouldn't let it go."

"She was there earlier tonight?" Bella was confused.

"Yep, you never saw her earlier because you were out like a light. But, she helped us get all the young girls into a van. That slimy Irish man took them to that rendezvous point—that's where we nabbed him. Jill was instrumental in that operation."

Mike cut him off. "I personally think Brian was hot for her. Never even questioned her story once."

Joseph laughed.

"I thought she was your girlfriend," Bella said to our driver.

"Nah, working this case is all, but guess we're good actors. We had everyone convinced."

I still wasn't connecting all the dots. "What was Uma's end game here?"

"Well, for one, she wanted to run the entire organization herself—she was highly jealous of Kali. Once she did away with Kali, she planned to launder money for who knows how long."

"Drugs, too?"

"Oh yeah. That's what Abram was brought in for. He's part of a worldwide cartel network. She seduced him … and he was ready to use Love & Mercy. It really is a perfect place to operate. Who suspects religious folks to be trafficking drugs?"

"Wow. And, I wanted to explore my spirituality and do a little self-help…" Bella shook her head. "I had no idea."

"Wait, Uma tried to kill Kali?" I asked. "And, earlier you said Uma buried my friends? Let's get back to that."

Joseph nodded, while glancing at Danny and Bella.

"And, you don't remember?" I asked the two.

"No," they said in unison.

"Then how'd they get to that cellar?" I asked Joseph and Mike.

Joseph cleared his throat. "When you ran off, Uma freaked out. She went from chanting devilish shit to barking orders. Brian had dumped Danny in a hole, then quickly grabbed Bella. He'd hooked some air tube, via the PVC pipe, to their mouths and started shoveling the dirt on them. I was horrified." He took a deep breath. "I never thought they'd *actually* do it. So, I told that red-headed bully I'd finish up. He and Uma should go find Abram. He'd gone running after you." After clearing his throat and taking a sip from his coffee cup, he continued. "Once they took off, I dug out Kali … Danny was partially covered in dirt, and they hadn't gotten around to throwing dirt on Bella yet."

"Hold on. Kali was buried there?"

He nodded sadly. "Yes. For the whole time—I didn't know; we'd been around that fire for a long time. I never saw her get buried, so I had no idea. Once I saw Brian set up that contraption for air, I realized what was protruding from the ground a few spots over. When I uncovered Kali…" Emotion took over and he dropped his head.

"So, where is she now?"

Joseph looked to Mike who then answered. "The hospital. I called for another security guard and asked him to get her to the hospital. He did; and thankfully neither Uma nor Brian knew a thing about that. By then, Uma was back at her residence—being seen by staff to establish an alibi and distancing herself from everything."

"And, you took them," pointing to Danny and Bella, "to the cellar, then?"

"Had to. I knew Brian was coming back since the whole plan was to move the immigrant girls during the night. All this other distraction was something I hadn't known about until late in the game. Anyway, by then, I knew Mike was keeping you out of the way until we could make our move. I had to make it seem as though I was working with Brian, or we'd have never made it out with all of you."

I was astonished at the level of complexity. Everything I thought I'd known earlier and all I was learning now. *Brian was capable of murder? How had I not seen that earlier?* My stomach started to churn. I thought he was my friend. He had been so nice to everyone around work.

CHAPTER THIRTY-FIVE

Once we made it back into the valley, Joseph and Mike dropped us off at our respective homes.

"Remember, three o'clock at the Mesa substation for statements. We'll meet you there," Joseph yelled out the window as Bella, Shadow, and I climbed out.

I'd never felt happier to walk in my front door. The second we did, my body felt limp and I dragged myself to the bedroom and plopped down on the bed. *When had I slept last?* I could hear the back door open—of course, Shadow needed out. I couldn't move though; Bella could handle it.

Hours later, I woke. Looking around, confused as to where I was, I smiled. *Ahhh, my room.* No more running off to yoga, meditation, or dodging slimy guys. My heart hurt then, thinking about Brian being one of them. I still couldn't imagine how I'd never detected his creepiness—even while at the retreat. He was one good character actor, that's for sure.

I got up and soaked in the bathtub for a long time. Laying there with my eyes closed, I wondered where Jill had gone. *Had she been at the huge police gathering in Patagonia?* I hadn't seen her. That seemed odd, but I suppose I didn't need to know every single move the agents made. I was still shocked that Joseph turned out to be one of the good guys. Why did Shadow always growl at him? Why did he send chills down my spine? Yet another great actor playing a part, I supposed.

Ah well, I knew something was going on with those people. And, I was right. As much as my friends get on me for snooping around, it was a good thing I had. Wait—I remembered that JJ and Joseph knew one another. I needed to ask JJ about that. *Oh, shoot ... I've gotta go buy a new phone. Ugh, I hate that process. Stupid Brian ...* that's when the image of him near the yurt, holding up a phone and saying he had to turn it in. That was *my* phone! My skin crawled, thinking that he'd been in our cabin while we were away.

* * *

Bella and I walked through the doors at the police station a few minutes before three that afternoon. In the light of day, all cleaned up now, and in a suit, Joseph wasn't near as scary as he'd been. He was actually quite handsome. Not that I was looking. Well, okay ... I had noticed; he was gorgeous. Why hadn't I appreciated that before? A tap on my shoulder and I turned around. Everyone else began following Joseph down the hallway.

"Hey sweetie, you okay?" Shock was etched onto my face I'm sure. Greg wrapped me up in his embrace. I broke down then—all the pent-up anxiety spilled out onto his shoulders. He held me tight until I finally raised my swollen eyes to his.

"When? How…" He shook his head and pulled me closer again. We stayed that way until Danny came down the hall and said they were waiting for us. Greg held my hand and we walked into a large conference room they were using as a holding area for our group. I introduced Greg to Danny. Then, Kali walked in. She was accompanied by a suited man I presumed to be her lawyer.

Over the course of a couple hours, we were shuffled individually to another small room and we each gave our statements. Greg accompanied me and I was thankful so I didn't have to repeat everything again later for him. It also helped to have a hand to hold.

While Bella was in the room with the officers, Kali turned to Danny. "I'm terribly saddened to learn about Emily. I had no idea, Danny."

Tears filled his eyes.

"I remember her well—she was the sweetest. Then after some time had passed, I stopped seeing her at the center. I'd asked Uma about her and she told me she had moved away. I had no idea."

Danny reached out for her hand, "I understand you had nothing to do with the actions of Uma and her cronies. Thank you for the kind words."

Kali admitted she needed to slow down, focus on the local center and stop playing in Hollywood. Maybe then she'd have seen the signs that were right under her nose.

She invited all of us to the center once this mess was behind us. She wanted to hold a proper celebration of life for Emily. Danny was touched, but I wasn't sure he ever wanted to step foot there again. I had the same sentiment.

It wasn't long before we'd all given our statements. We thanked Kali for her kindness, and Danny promised to think about the celebration of life for Emily. She offered each of us lifelong memberships for us and our families—for courses, retreats, all of it. It was clear she felt horrible about what her second in command had been doing behind her back. She felt responsible for not seeing or stopping it sooner, but she related how it was her every intention to make it up to her members and move forward carefully when selecting leaders for the organization.

"Wanna stop in at the spa on the way home?" I turned to Bella as we climbed into my 4Runner.

"Sure. But, not for long. I'm exhausted still ... even after a nap."

I waved to Greg, who'd parked next to us, and shouted for him to follow us to the spa. My sentiments were the same—keep it short—but I really wanted to check in with Lexi. She had left several messages after she heard through JJ about the bust.

* * *

It turned out my mother and my sister, Jordan, were at the spa also when we got there. They'd had appointments with Kathleen and Diane apparently. I was quite surprised, but it made it easier to tell everyone at once, so I endured.

In the Serenity Room, we relaxed with hot tea and a background of calming music. They all listened intently as we retold the entire retreat story. Each time I spoke of things like micro-dosing and burial, it seemed more surreal. The look on each family member's face was reflective of what we'd been through. But, regardless of our horrors, imagine the young girls that had been trafficked through their facility for how many years … five? How disgusting. The images from the night they drugged me at that party. Now I realized exactly what I'd seen in those dark corners.

Jordan was shocked that Senator Maizer was caught up in it. She had been his date for the gratitude educational session weeks back and said he was a perfect gentleman. She'd hoped he'd call her again for a date. Not anymore.

CHAPTER THIRTY-SIX

Two weeks later, I got a call from Danny. The celebration of life was to be held that weekend for Emily and he asked us to join him. We knew how much it'd mean to him so we agreed and I asked if I could bring a plus-one. Thankfully, Greg was back from his assignment in New Mexico and we'd already planned to spend a long-awaited weekend together. He was gracious enough to agree to join us for Danny's daughter's memorial.

Bella, Joseph, Mike, Greg, and I all walked through the huge front doors of Love & Mercy at two Saturday afternoon. Greg was the only one who had not been to any of their facilities and the awestruck look indicated he was impressed. The fountains, the lighted statues, everything was perfect. Bella and I hesitated momentarily as one of the ushers held up a tray of juice shots. Then we both smiled at the kind gentleman simultaneously and decided we were safe; we'd go ahead and enjoy the sweet treat. I noticed that neither Joseph nor Mike indulged.

"Oh, that was good..." Greg commented, none the wiser, as we walked across the bridge toward the auditorium. Bella and I winked at one another, deciding that the past was behind us now and we no longer needed to worry about being micro-dosed. Those responsible were now in jail.

Danny saw us from across the room and made his way over. With a huge smile, he gave Bella and me each a hug.

"Thank you for coming here today. This means so much to me." He reached out to shake hands with Greg, Joseph, and the enormous security guard who no longer appeared terribly frightening. "Without your help, I probably would still be seeking answers for my daughter's death. It's still not easy to admit she committed suicide, but I'm relieved to know that those responsible are behind bars. I'll always be grateful to you."

"You have yourself to acknowledge too, man," Mike pointed out. "You, Libby, and that brave dog of hers. You led us to those criminals and participated in a way that gave us an airtight case. They won't be seeing the outside of prison, probably for the rest of their lives. Thank *you*."

Kali walked up and hugged us all. "Welcome! So happy to see you all. We're going to have a nice program in place today to honor Emily. Take your seats and I'll go round up everyone who hasn't crossed the bridge yet. Let's get this thing started."

Before I sat, I saw Katie in the doorway. I waved for her to come sit with us, and she did. Jordan also found her way to us and so had Jill, who was busy chatting with Joseph.

I hadn't met her before, so we quickly greeted each other, and I introduced everyone else before the lights dimmed.

Kali settled the room with her soothing voice, leading us through a short guided meditation filled with loving words. Tears gently snuck out the corner of my eyes as she spoke of those who had passed before us—appreciating all we've learned from them. My thoughts went to my father, who had died when I was only a teen. Oh, how I'd missed him through the years and wished he'd been there to guide me. I remembered all the camping and fishing we'd done in my youth—he was my first true outdoorsman who'd taught me the value of nature and how to respect it.

After the meditation, Kali expertly guided numerous family members and those that knew Emily from the church to come up and speak about her. So many stories were told—laughter and tears continued for the next hour. Danny was the last to speak. His heartfelt words for his daughter gripped my heart. I was fortunate to have met this man.

The universe works in mysterious ways, but the friendship we've forged now has shown that he descended to me right from heaven. The exact thing I needed in my life when I didn't even realize I needed it. He'd never be a replacement for my father, but we could certainly help each other with those pieces from our heart that were abruptly taken from us. We'd both come to that determination when we chose to accept the lifetime membership and continue the journey of healing and growing.

The reception following the memorial was nothing short of grand—of course it was, that's what Kali does best. Tuxedoed men and women strolled the room with mouth-watering appetizers and fruity drinks.

A lady tapped me on the shoulder as I stood talking with Greg.

"Libby?" she questioned meekly.

I saw a dark-haired woman with gray streaks running through. "Yes…"

"I'm Bonnie's mom, Cheryl Wallace."

My mouth flew open; I reached out and pulled her into hug. "I'm so happy to meet you! I had no idea you'd be here."

"Danny invited us all. He also said you were instrumental in getting to the bottom of…" her voice choked, "of … Bonnie's death."

I squeezed her into a hug again. "I'm *so sorry* for your loss."

She pushed back, taking my hands into hers, and looked into my eyes. "Your friend, Joseph … I just talked with him, he also said you had helped bring down those monsters. Thank you."

"Oh, I don't know that it was me…" I sheepishly hung my head.

"And your dog! They said Shadow stopped them from doing even worse things!"

"Well, let's say that there were several of us—but most importantly, the FBI."

She was shaking her head and finger-wagged in front of my face. "No. The FBI have been working for *years* on this. Slow as molasses. Had they figured it out sooner, my Bonnie would be alive. I thank you for being brave enough to keep asking the hard questions. And, doing what's *right*. We need that more in our society."

"Yes, I agree with law enforcement needing to speed things up. How'd…" I stopped myself, my eyes finding the floor, flushing with embarrassment as I realized how inappropriate I'd almost been. What I really was curious about was *how* Bonnie had died, but it seemed rude to ask outright. My eyes cautiously looked into hers. She understood.

"She was poisoned," Cheryl said softly. "I'd heard something about psychedelics being used at the retreat?"

I nodded. "Thank you, I've wondered what toxicology found. I'd heard she had…"

"Epilepsy, yes. But this wasn't that. She choked on vomit when she had an adverse reaction to the drugs … and, well, she aspirated. They tried hard to save her in the hospital—but she'd been without oxygen too long. Died of asphyxiation." She used her tissue to wipe the tears from her eyes.

"I'm so sorry. I didn't know her at all, but I wish…"

"It's okay, Libby. From all I've heard, you've saved others from those maniacs. That's what's most important."

"Have you learned *why* they went after Bonnie? Had she gotten too close to the truth, do you think?"

"I have no idea why they killed my baby," she sobbed. I wrapped by arms around her and let her cry.

Katie walked up and took my place with hugs. Greg and I said our goodbyes to them and began to mingle with others.

Joseph wandered over to where we admired the waterfall cascading from the second story.

Greg looked over at him. "Gorgeous, huh?"

"Kali sure knows how to make people comfortable—all their places are beautifully designed."

I was curious, "I know Uma, Abram, Brian, and the senator are all in jail. But, how far and wide had these criminals infiltrated Kali's organization? Are there others you're still investigating?"

"Within Love & Mercy, no. We've got them. However, all of them also face federal crimes—this is not the only place they were laundering and trafficking. It's a huge world-wide network. We got these three and hopefully they'll cooperate to help us bring down the entire network. We'll see. So far, they aren't being all that cooperative."

"I keep thinking to that night they invited me to the yurt party. What was the purpose of that? Why would they want me there if they were skeptical of me?"

Joseph shrugged. "Keep your enemies close, I guess? I don't really know. But, whatever they drugged you with that night was also what was used on Bonnie. It killed Bonnie. So…"

Greg gripped my hand tighter. "I hope they fry," he told Joseph.

I turned to Joseph. "Do you know who took me home that night? That still freaks me out a little."

"I did. I picked you up from the dance floor and then called Badri." Visions of large hands reaching toward me. That made sense. I looked at his face—five o'clock shadow; that's what I felt.

"Badri! Please tell me he wasn't any part of this…"

"He wasn't."

"Thank God! He was so nice, but by that last day I had no idea who I could trust. It's probably a good thing that I hadn't known you were there. I probably would have run." We both laughed heartily, knowing that's exactly what would have happened.

"I had you pretty frightened, didn't I?"

I nodded in agreement, and then turned to JJ. "Hey, my

friend. I didn't know you'd be here. Where's the family?"

He was already shaking hands and doing the bro-hug with Greg and Joseph. He pointed to Joseph as he answered. "This guy told me about this. Sorry I'm late. Lex and Joshua are at home. Hopefully you'll stop over sometime this weekend?"

I looked to Greg and we both nodded—that sounded like a plan.

"Hey Joseph, what have we learned about Healing Solutions?" JJ inquired.

That got my attention. Of course, Brian worked there ... was he involved in criminal activity there also?

"Looks like it was a legit job for him. He needed cover; I guess he was fearful we were on to him. Yeah, we found that outside of his involvement with Abram, he is legitimately a physical therapist. Well, *was* ... those days are over for him."

I shook my head, staring at the ground. "He was a good one, too. It's a shame." I looked up and caught Greg's smirk. "I thought we were friends. I'm still shocked he tried to harm me ... and my friends. Never saw that coming."

JJ and Joseph continued to talk shop. I looked around the room and saw that a few people had left but most were enjoying their time with friends and family. A server approached with a tray of drinks. Again, I paused when the pink champagne glasses were presented to me. I laughed to myself and picked up the beautiful flute. Greg did the same.

He winked at me, "To the most adventurous girl I know. I've missed you, Libby Madsen." He clinked his glass with mine.

"I've missed you, too, Greg Lawson."

We leaned in and kissed each other, forgetting all about those around us. Just the hunky forest ranger and the massage therapist lost in each other for a few seconds before we were brought back into reality. Long distance relationships may be difficult, but I was bound and determined to keep this man in my life.

What's next for Libby and Shadow?

Jerome is an old mining town turned hipster tourist destination in Arizona. An old friend, Kirby McDaniel, calls Libby asking for help filling in at her massage business in the town's haunted hotel. Libby is reluctant at first, but when she learns Greg has time off as well, they decide to use the opportunity to also make this a well-needed short romantic getaway. Kirby's cute cottage is the perfect location for rest and relaxation so Libby, Greg, and Shadow pack their bags, eager to explore the area.

However, upon arriving in the small-town community, they meet the eclectic Cheryl Basque who they learn is the Murder Mystery Weekend coordinator. Apparently, MMW is the event of the year in Jerome. Kirby failed to mention this to Libby—she had signed up and now with her sudden departure, the coordinator finds herself in a bind. The full-court press is on to lure Libby and Greg to join the festivities in Kirby's absence. Shadow is suspicious of the pushy lady.

In the meantime, Libby meets interesting townsfolk in the massage therapy room. The bakery owner, the brew master duo, the hotel manager, and MMW's coordinator have one thing in common. They all have had issues with the local dog groomer. That only becomes a problem once the hated groomer, Patricia Olivia Simpson, turns up murdered.

Between therapy sessions, participating in the murder mystery game, being spooked by hotel ghosts, and running down a list of suspects who all had the motive to kill Tricia, will Libby and Greg actually find the much-needed time together? Through many twists and turns, Libby, Greg, and Shadow find themselves in the adventure of a lifetime in *Spooky Shadows*.

Thank you for taking the time to read *Shadow Retreats*.
If you enjoyed it please tell your friends, and I would be
so grateful if you would consider posting a review.
Word of mouth is an author's best friend, and very
much appreciated.
Thank you,
Jennifer Morgan

* * *

**Get another free book from Jennifer—Scan the
QR code and visit her website to find out how!**

Books in the Libby Madsen series:
Shadows in the Forest
Spa Shadows
Shadowed Treasures
Shadow Retreats
The Christmas Fairy – a holiday novella

Let's connect!
Website: jenniferjmorgan.com
Email: jennifer@jenniferjmorgan.com
Facebook: facebook.com/profile.
php?id=100076154359528
Twitter: JenniferJMorga3
BookBub: bookbub.com/profile/433830544
Goodreads: goodreads.com/user/show/148099219-
jennifer-morgan

www.ingramcontent.com/pod-product-compliance
Lightning Source LLC
Chambersburg PA
CBHW050201120726
47903CB00002B/718